The Hienama

A Story of the Sulh

A Wraeththu Mythos Novel

The Hienama

A Story of the Sulh

A Wraeththu Mythos Novel

Storm Constantine

IMMANION
PRESS
Stafford England

http://www.stormconstantine.com

Cover Design by Storm Constantine
Cover Art by Ruby
Interior Layout/Design by Storm Constantine

Set in Souvenir

IP0027

An Immanion Press Edition
8 Rowley Grove
Stafford ST17 9BJ
UK

http://www.immanion-press.com
info@immanion-press.com

ISBN 978-1-904853-62-6

Books by Storm Constantine

The Wraeththu Chronicles
*The Enchantments of Flesh and Spirit
*The Bewitchments of Love and Hate
*The Fulfilments of Fate and Desire
*The Wraeththu Chronicles (omnibus of trilogy)

The Artemis Cycle
The Monstrous Regiment
Aleph

*Hermetech
Burying the Shadow
Sign for the Sacred
Calenture
Thin Air

The Grigori Books
*Stalking Tender Prey
*Scenting Hallowed Blood
*Stealing Sacred Fire

Silverheart (with Michael Moorcock)

The Magravandias Chronicles:
Sea Dragon Heir
Crown of Silence
The Way of Light

The Wraeththu Histories:
*The Wraiths of Will and Pleasure
*The Shades of Time and Memory
*The Ghosts of Blood and Innocence

Wraeththu Mythos
*Student of Kyme

Short Story Collections:
The Thorn Boy and Other Dreams of Dark Desire
*Mythanima
*available as Immanion Press editions

1

The whole experience was different for me, because I came to Wraeththu pretty late. In comparison. Most of the hara around me had been incepted in their teens, whereas I was in my early twenties when it happened. I always felt kind of out of place because of that. Not that hara weren't good to me. It wasn't that. I just had memories they didn't have.

I'd been incepted into the Sulh, a travelling band, and the har who came to me after althaia told me that magic was strong in me, and that I should go to the town of Jesith to find instruction. A hienama there was renowned among the Sulh. His name was Ysobi.

Jesith was a village rather than a town, stuck on a bleak cliff on the northwest coast of the Alba Sulh phylarchy of Lyonis. Its former human inhabitants had been wiped out by a plague that had struck there ten years ago, or so. Most of Alba Sulh had been ravaged by plagues and the humans who'd survived them had either fled to the eastern continent or had settled uncomfortably into a kind of barbaric feudalism; small groups fending off the depredations of rogue Wraeththu groups. The Sulh, and other smaller tribes of civilised ways, tried to mediate and soothe any conflict, but since neither the humans nor the rogue hara had any particular interest in forging peace, this was difficult to police.

I had heard stories of how hara had come into Jesith by night, when fog had lain thick over the hills, making everything seem haunted and silent. There had still been lights burning in some of the windows, but as the hara stole between the buildings, like phantoms of mist themselves, and had looked between the open curtains, they'd found only abandonment or death. They'd cleared the corpses away and taken over the place for themselves. They renamed it, of course.

I turned up one afternoon in the late summer, having travelled there on foot from a larger settlement in the north. I'd been har for a few years by then, having taken a while to accept what my early friend had told me. At first, I'd been interested only in my new condition, my physical self. All that I'd been before seemed like a nightmare, a fever dream. I could remember what I'd been like, but only in the way you can remember stories you read in a newspaper. I'd discovered I was intelligent, full of curiosity and – most surprisingly – somewhat sensitive. What I'd been before I preferred not to think about. I'd been dragged to inception roaring and fighting, and now I couldn't get enough of looking at myself, thinking: I am *this*, I really am. After three years or so, the novelty had still not worn off.

I walked round Jesith a couple of times, to get my bearings, then went to the largest inn for a different kind of information. It was called Willow Pool Garden, because, yes, it had a garden, a pool and willows at the back. The place was nearly empty, but there were two young hara in there, pale-skinned and dark-haired as I was. They spotted me as a stranger straight away and came directly to the table where I'd chosen to sip my ale. The beer was heavy and thick, very sweet; I found out later honey was involved in its production. 'What have you come here for?' one of them asked, 'nohar hardly ever comes *here.*' He said this in the way the young have always spoken of their hometowns; disparagingly, and aghast that strangers would find their way there. That amused me. Some things never change.

'I've come to ask a hienama here, Ysobi, for training,' I answered.

The two hara exchanged a glance, rolled their eyes, and laughed. 'Ah,' they said in unison.

I raised my eyebrows in enquiry.

'That's the only reason anyhar would ever come here,' one of them explained, helpfully. 'I suppose Yzzi is a legend.'

'I heard he's good,' I said.

'Somehar must think *you* are, then.' The har shook his head, and held out his hand, which seemed an oddly archaic gesture. 'Sorry, I'm Minnow.' He jerked his head towards his companion. 'He's Vole. We were twins, well, still are...'

Two little creatures; quick Minnow and shy Vole. They were to become friends of mine. I took Minnow's hand and shook it. 'Hi, I'm Jassenah.'

'We can show you to the Nayati in a little while,' Minnow said. 'Yzzi is in charge of it. There are a couple of other hienamas, who deal with any inceptions and basic caste training, but Yzzi is the specialist. He has a lot of students come to him from other phyles. He's picky. He has to be. But I'm sure he'll take you on.'

'I don't know how I'll be able to pay him, supposing there is a charge.'

'Most students find work here while they're training, or their own phyle makes some kind of donation to Jesith, but if Yzzi thinks you're worth it, he'll do it for free. It's his vocation.'

I was intrigued.

There was an old church in the town, but it had fallen mostly into ruins. The hara there had built their own Nayati, in wood. It consisted of a main hall, with tiers of seats down two sides, which were supported on thick pillars, so that there was standing room underneath. The floor was inlaid with symbols. At the far end were ritual rooms for inceptions and other rites, and there was an extension on the right side, which was Ysobi's small college. Nohar actually lived there with him. Students were given accommodation in the town and any other hienamas attached to the Nayati also lived elsewhere. There were still a lot of empty dwellings in Jesith. At that time, any newcomer could take their pick.

Minnow led me down the Nayati to an arched wooden door, silent Vole lingering behind us. The afternoon had faded. I could smell the aroma of cooking meat as the inhabitants of Jesith prepared their evening meals. Minnow knocked on the door and without waiting for a response, opened it. I followed him into the room beyond.

The first thing I saw was the domed cage, in which two brightly coloured birds flickered round like jewels. The floor was mostly covered in cushions, and where there were no cushions there were papers, books, arcane equipment and other paraphernalia associated with the dedicated magus. Ysobi himself, or the har I took to be him, sat on one of the cushions, examining what looked like an essay. He was frowning a little and didn't look up immediately.

'Yzzi,' Minnow said. 'This har has been sent to you.'

The hienama looked up then. I don't know what I had expected really, but he wasn't quite up to whatever nebulous expectations I'd had. Perhaps already I assumed that Wraeththu legends were all great beauties, who could entrance with a single glance. Ysobi wasn't ugly, of course, but I remember thinking he was too gaunt. His hair was very long, but rather lank, as if he hadn't washed it for a while. He was dressed in a dark robe with a hood, and his face was bony. High cheekbones, grey hollows beneath them. Deep-set eyes, a long thin nose and rather full lips, which looked strange in juxtaposition with the rest of his features. I thought he was odd-looking, and that he could do with a good feed and a long bath. He smiled as I stared at him, and I felt myself flush; it was as if he'd read my thoughts, which of course he probably had. Part of why I was there was to learn how to control and best use my abilities.

'How can I help you?' he asked me, in a voice that was in fact quite beautiful.

'The hara who incepted me advised me to come here,' I said, suddenly feeling I was about to look stupid for imagining I was something more than I was. 'They recommended you.'

'And what is there about you to recommend?' he asked reasonably.

I wanted to shrug and mutter something non-committal, but sensed this would not be the best course. 'They thought I needed training different to the one they could give me. I'm untried. I don't know if they're right. But I came here, all the same.'

Ysobi nodded once and carefully put down the papers he'd been reading. 'Minnow, you can go now. Come back in two hours, then find our guest somewhere to stay.'

'You'll take me on?' I asked, quite surprised it had been that easy.

'I didn't say that, but presumably you don't plan on moving on again tonight, in any case.'

'I'm sorry... yes, I mean no. Sorry.'

Ysobi smiled mildly. 'It's quite all right.'

Minnow patted my arm. 'We'll come back later, then,' he said. 'Show you around, find you a bed.'

'Thank you.'

After Minnow had gone, Ysobi gestured with one hand. 'Put down your bag. Please, sit down.'

I did so. 'I should have sent a message to you,' I said. 'I feel a bit bad now, just turning up.'

'I'm under no obligation and difficult to embarrass,' Ysobi said.

I felt mortified, but then he laughed.

'Relax. We'll talk. It's not a case of you being good enough for me; it's whether I think I can help you. Would you like tea? It's flavoured with cinnamon. Some hara don't like it.'

'That'd be fine.'

He took a cloth off the pot that stood on the low table before him and poured some of the amber fluid into two delicate cups that had no handles. I had never tasted tea like that before. I really liked it. Just the scent of cinnamon nowadays takes me back to that day.

'How long have you been har?' Ysobi asked.

'About three years.'

'And what level are you at in your training?'

I shrugged. 'Well, I had basic instruction after inception. I suppose I'm just Ara. The hara who incepted me were basically farmers, not mystics.'

'But Sulh, though?'

'Yes, Sulh.' Most hara who weren't, in this country, were regarded as vagabonds, looters and pirates.

'How old were you at inception?'

'Twenty-two.'

Ysobi nodded slowly. 'Hmm.'

'Is that bad?'

'No, not especially. Training perhaps comes easier to the young, because they have fewer preconceptions.'

'That goes for everything to do with being har,' I said, before I'd had time to consider the words.

'That, of course, is why most hara are incepted young. What's your story?'

I had to turn my gaze away from his eyes. 'I was born in a northern city. I ran wild. I'm not proud of what I was. I prefer to forget it.'

'I would like to know how you came to be incepted.'

'We were...' I rubbed my face. 'I was part of a gang whose sole aim in life was to terrorise Wraeththu. We were an irritant, tolerated for only so long. When the hara struck back, they did so swiftly and expediently. We didn't stand a chance. Those who weren't killed were incepted. I was one of the survivors.'

'How long did you live that life, before you became har?'

'About four years. Too long.'

'You were no street kid, I can see that.'

'I left my home. It was more than rebellion. The world was ending.'

Ysobi nodded again. I wanted to ask him how *he* had come to be incepted too. He was talking to me as if he'd never been human.

'The main thing I've learned since inception,' I said, 'is that I have a mind. I have opinions. I never did before. But I used to take a lot of drugs...' I raised my hands. 'You don't need me to tell you.'

'You have adjusted well, in my opinion,' Ysobi said. 'More tea?'

I held out my cup. 'I'm not unhappy. I'm not fucked up. That's not why I'm here.'

'Then why are you here?'

'To learn. I want to learn. I've been reading a lot.'

Ysobi laughed, but not unkindly. 'You are quite the butterfly, aren't you, or should I say swan?'

I wondered if he was being sarcastic. 'I could have been dead. I'm not. I've been given another chance. If that's being a butterfly or a swan, then yes.'

Ysobi stared at me unblinkingly. 'They incepted you because they could tell you could take it. Not many your age could. It drives men mad. It either makes them more violent, in denial, or they become drooling idiots. The adjustments they have to make are vast.'

'It's not a fate worse than death.'

'Some think it is.'

'Well, I'm not one of them.'

Ysobi gave me a shrewd look then, which I resented, because I thought he believed I was deluding myself. I thought he believed I was in denial. What could I say? I'd been prejudged.

He let the silence hang there between us for a while, sipping his tea, his gaze blank. I was thinking I should get out of there, wondering how to do it without looking a worse idiot. Eventually, I said, 'Tiahaar, if you'd prefer me to leave, I will.'

'What?' He looked surprised at the sound of my voice, as if he'd forgotten I was there.

'I said...'

'I heard what you said. Excuse me, I was thinking.'

I sat there for some moments, wondering how much pleasure he got from playing the guru. It had been a mistake to come here.

'We can start now,' he said, glancing up at me. 'If that's OK with you?'

I blinked at him. 'Well...'

'What is your name?'

'Jass... Jassenah.'

'Jassenah har Sulh.'

I nodded.

'I'd like to run through some basic tests, just to see where you're at. Nothing too strenuous.'

'And after that, you'll decide whether to take me on?'

He smiled. 'I've already decided that.'

Minnow and Vole found me a cottage near the centre

of town. It was close to the narrow harbour, which was situated in a short estuary with high cliffs to either side. A fast-moving river rushed only a few yards from my front door, but behind the cottage was a field with sheep in it. More fields, dotted with copses of ancient trees, led to dark forests. The cottage was pretty run down, but the plumbing worked and it was hooked to the main town generator. It had two rooms downstairs and a kitchen with a wood-burning stove in it. Upstairs were two bedrooms and a rather unsavoury bathroom. In the larger of the rooms, there was a bed, which was a bit mouldy, but Minnow said he knew somehar who had a spare mattress. 'Well, he makes them, actually, but he'll usually give one for free to a newcomer. Don't suppose you've got much to barter with.'

'Not much,' I agreed.

'We'll have to find you some work too,' Minnow said, 'supposing you want to eat, and so on.'

'What's on offer?'

'Well, Jesith's main produce is wine, of just about every variety. Other towns say we can make it from dead rats, but that's not strictly true.' He grinned. 'We save the odd rat for the best vintage! No, I'm joking. Anyway, I work at the vineyard. I'll take you tomorrow. Sinnar's a decent har. He runs it. He's also our phylarch.'

'OK, sounds fine to me.'

'You can eat with us tonight, if you want.'

'Thanks.'

That first evening, Vole cooked for Minnow and me. They lived in another cottage quite near to mine, and I was impressed at what they'd done with it. I didn't know how long I'd remain in Jesith, but basking in the delights of physical comfort, I resolved to do my cottage up a little and make it cosier.

After dinner, the twins took me out to show me what happened in Jesith after dark. There were several bars, which most hara visited at least once each evening. Food was available, and a variety of liquors from Sinnar's yard, including ale. I got to meet some of the local celebrities. It was interesting.

It was then I first met Zehn, in a bar called The Leaping Cat. It was despite at first sight. I'd seen his type a hundred times before: the golden har who everyhar desires, and who knows it. He was beautiful, of course, with hair the colour of ripe wheat. It hung over his face and he kept pushing it back, aware of how lovely it was. He had some hapless soul with him, a red-haired beauty, who was no doubt attached for the duration of the evening and not far beyond. Zehn spent a few minutes trying to flirt with me, much to the distress of his companion, but I wouldn't bite.

'You're new,' he drawled, expecting me to be entranced.

I uttered a kind of grunt in response. I'd been bitten once or twice, in places very tender, by hara of his kind. I'd learned to see beyond the surface; usually, beneath was rot. His strategy would be to seduce every new face in town, then discard them. Pathetic, really.

'He's training with Ysobi,' Minnow supplied.

Zehn laughed. 'Good luck.'

I didn't think I needed luck. The preliminary exercises had gone well with Ysobi that afternoon. I thought he'd been pleased with me. Clearly, a har of Zehn's type would never consider taking any kind of training. It was beneath me to respond.

'You're not one of those serious souls, are you?' Zehn asked me, grinning.

'You're not one of those superficial ones, are you?' I replied, smiling sweetly.

'Ow, claws!' he said.

'Sheathed at the moment, I assure you.' I decided it was time to move on.

Minnow and Vole were happy to show me somewhere different. As we went out into the street, Minnow said, 'I think Zehn likes you.'

'I think he likes everyhar,' I said. 'Not my type at all.'

Minnow laughed. 'What is your type? Do you want to find him tonight?'

'No. I want to get my bearings here before anything else.'

'Zehn made you angry,' Vole said. 'You didn't need to get mad at him.' He rarely spoke, so the comment stung.

'I know his kind,' I said. 'Really, I'm not angry. I just don't like hara thinking I'm stupid.'

'Let's go to Willow Pool Garden,' Minnow said, so we went.

Like most Sulh communities at that time, Jesith ran mostly on bartering systems, although the phylarch, Sinnar, paid us in coins that could be redeemed at the few shops and bars. It was a kind of credit system for his hara. These tokens could also be bought from Sinnar with other goods, whether they were logs from the forest, trout from the river or wild blackberries from the heath for his wine vats. He'd set up commerce with other local phylarchs, so his tokens could be used widely in the area. Everyhar called them 'sins,' which amused him. Sinnar had been incepted further north in one of the cities, and had come south, after being trained in Kyme, to take over the phyle. Like most Kyme hara, he was fond of knowledge but, unlike your usual Kymian, far from ascetic. I guess he couldn't have run a vineyard otherwise. He was the kind of har that is almost too easy on the eye; tawny hair, generous even features and sensitive hands. His manner was both composed and competent. A born leader, I guess.

Sinnar agreed to interview me at Minnow's request, but I could tell it was merely a formality. The phylarch was keen to expand his business, so new workers were always welcome. As Minnow led me through the busy workshops and yard to Sinnar's office, I wondered how my training would fit in around a physical job.

Minnow left me sitting in the office and after a few minutes, Sinnar came in, poring through a huge ledger. He appeared distracted, more interested in the entries in his ledger than in me. He sat down and closed his book, folding his hands together on the desk top.

'You're here to train with Ysobi,' Sinnar said.

'Yes, but I need to work. I don't know much about making wine, but I'm willing to learn.'

Sinnar nodded, sucked his upper lip. 'Fine. You have somewhere to stay?'

'Yes, Minnow and Vole found me a cottage.'

'Excellent. Well, you'll obviously need to spend some time each day on your studies, so how about you come to the yard each morning at eight o'clock and work for four hours? Weekends off, unless we have a lot on.'

'That sounds very generous.'

Sinnar smiled. 'I don't believe in working hara too hard, and I expect Ysobi will give you a lot to do.' He paused. 'You know of his reputation, of course?'

I displayed my palms. 'It's why I'm here. He was recommended.'

Sinnar nodded. He had an introspective look to him, which made me wonder what he was thinking. Did he think I wasn't of high enough calibre for Ysobi to teach me?

'Shall I start work now?' I asked.

Sinnar collected himself. 'Yes, by all means do. Go and find Minnow. He'll show you around.'

And that was that: I had a job.

For three weeks, Ysobi went over basic training in various skills with me, such as far-seeing, psychic communication and healing. He taught me to be more sensitive to the energy of the universe, which the Sulh had named agmara, and how to manipulate it to create effects in reality. He was a patient and humorous teacher, but somehow distant. I never saw him outside of his Nayati, other than in the garden that surrounded the building on three sides. Sometimes we took lessons out there. If he had other students, I didn't meet them. I trained with him for three hours a day, every afternoon. Before and after that, I worked for Sinnar. I'd been employed to work only mornings, but because things were so busy, I usually ended up going back to the vineyard after my training to help out with deliveries and so on. This meant I earned extra, so I wasn't unhappy about it.

Jesith was a stable and close community, mainly because Sinnar was such a stable and open kind of har. They had trouble occasionally with rogues trying to loot crops and supplies, so there was a town guard that patrolled the borders and kept any rabble at bay. Zehn, I learned, was one of these guards. I imagine the tenuous glamour of that role had appealed to him.

I worked on my cottage and also acquired a pony, which lived with the sheep in the field behind my home. I began to build up a social life, revolving around the friends of Minnow and Vole, but something prevented me from initiating intimacy with anyhar I met. It wasn't that there weren't hara I liked, there were, but perhaps the intensive training stunted my sensuality. I don't know. Maybe it was something else, a precognition.

The reason I say this is that a few weeks into the training, Ysobi announced that before I progressed any further, he must teach me the arunic arts, how to use aruna as magic. I'd always known this could be done, but imagined it was a private thing between hara working together magically. I said this. Ysobi told me it could be that way, but unless I knew what I was doing I would be an impediment to any har who might want to work with me, and who knows, there might come a day when proper training would save somehar's life.

We were in his main room, which I noticed he'd tidied up a little. My mouth went dry. I felt apprehensive. The day was overcast, but humid. Later, there would be thunder. 'What do you want me to do?' I asked.

'Sit down,' he said, indicating one of the cushions.

I did so and he sat cross-legged before me. He wound his hair into a rope and tied it in a loose knot at the nape of his neck.

'Take my hands.'

I reached out to him, and his palms were dry and very hot in the centres.

'Close your eyes, Jassenah. Good. I want you to extend your senses, become aware of my energy field. Can you do that?'

'Yes...' It was like a tingle. I could feel energy streaming up my arms from his hands.

'Take it down into your body. Concentrate it in the lower belly.'

It went down as heat, like taking in a hot drink.

'We must breathe together, in through the nose and out through the mouth, totally synchronised. Now focus.'

Even though our faces were some distance apart, it was almost like sharing breath. I took him into me, down into my lungs. I could feel my body stirring, like an animal waking up and sniffing around. He kept the breathing going for some time, until I felt light-headed. Then he withdrew his hands from mine, and it made me dizzy. I felt as if I was hanging alone in a void, spinning. It was euphoric and disorientating.

Gently, he pushed me back onto the floor cushions. 'Relax, Jassenah. Do nothing but concentrate on your breathing. Keep it steady.'

I felt his hands at my belt. He undressed me as a healer might; efficiently and quickly. I felt cold then, despite the humid air. He raised my knees and parted my legs, leaving me feeling vulnerable and exposed. I didn't want him looking at me, but was powerless to move. He put a towel beneath me.

'There are five energy centres within the soume-lam,' he said. 'They are called sikras. I'm going to activate the first two, perhaps the third. While I do this, focus your mind on that area of your body. Pay attention to sensation. This is not for pleasure.'

I was lying there with my eyes closed, tense as a wire. I expected him to use his fingers, but he didn't. He used his tongue. What I learned first that day was that all aruna I'd experienced to date had been fairly basic. I'd been ouana and rooned hara, and I'd been soume and they'd rooned me, but I'd done nothing like this. It was electrifying. I hadn't even known about sikras, since all aruna to me had been one heady, intoxicating experience. No har I'd been with had ever been this precise. Ysobi stimulated the first sikra until it swelled into a bud. I could feel it and the sensation was incredible. I don't think it had ever happened to me before, or if it had, I hadn't noticed. I felt as if I was on the brink of an out-of-body experience. Then he went a little deeper inside and ignited a second fire within me. I had to make some noise, and all thoughts of breathing regularly flew up the chimney. Ysobi slowly ran his tongue over the two swollen sikras a few times and then reached for the third. Even though I felt drunk, I could tell that each sikra had a slightly different feeling, like a sound or a taste. The third one was a distant itch he could just about reach. I was so beside myself with desire, I pushed down on him. Was this arousing him too? I couldn't tell.

Then he drew away from me. I lay there gasping

for a few moments, my entire soume-lam contracting with need.

'Focus,' Ysobi said softly. 'Feel the energy of it. Feel it circling. Try to contain it.'

I thought he was mad. How could such a thing be possible? Was he going to leave me like this? I opened my eyes and looked at him. He was kneeling between my legs, wiping his mouth with the back of one hand. He smiled at me. 'Hang on to that power, let it build within you. Don't let it dissipate. When we reach the peak of release, you must send it out as a spear of intention. For now, you can just send it out for the good of Jesith and its hara. Just release it, as if it's a bird that's going to fly from your body. Do you understand?'

I must have nodded or made a sound. Ysobi lifted his robe and I had a brief glimpse of his erect ouana-lim. Then he leaned forward and pulled me towards him, his hands at the base of my spine. I felt him touch me, and now his eyes were closed, while mine were open. I wanted to see him go into me, if I could, I don't know why, but the robe was in the way, as if he was modest. He entered me very slowly, almost teasing. He was hot and very hard, pushing through the soft yet swollen folds of me, pushing past the pulsing buds, stimulating them further. It was as if I had eyes inside myself. He filled me utterly and I could feel every part of him, even though I was so drenched with my own fluids and his saliva. I was frantic for him to go deeper, but he held on to my hips firmly to stop me moving too much and took his time. Once he was buried in me entirely, he remained still. I could feel his heart beating through his ouana-lim, I could hear the soft rush of blood. My fingers clenched on air at my sides, like a cat marking time.

Ysobi took a deep breath, then withdrew from me, nearly all the way. It was like the tide going out. Part of me was drawn out with him. Then he pushed back in, in a swift deep plunge. The sikras inside me were almost shrieking. His movements became deep and regular. He released his hold on my hips a little so I could move with him. I wanted to drag him down, feel his weight upon me, hold him close, but he was beyond my reach. We just connected at the groin, with my legs around his waist. I can remember every moment of it. I can close my eyes and relive the entire experience in detail. I can remember the power building up, as if my own release was a tidal wave surging towards me. Exquisite feelings burst like fireworks, flowers turning into sparks, sparks turning into flowers. When the inner tongue of his ouana-lim snaked out, I felt it make contact with the fifth centre inside me. I think what happens is that this tendril actually penetrates the flesh of the centre. That's what it felt like, anyway. He was in me, but then he was *in* me in a different way. There was a roar in my head, and the wave crashed over me, catching me in its maelstrom, throwing me against rocks. The contractions were so intense, it was almost painful, yet the most delicious pleasure I had ever experienced. Aruna is often like a pageant of visions, but this was so physical. Ysobi's voice was in my head: *Jassenah, now! Direct it!* It was almost too late, but somehow I caught it by the tail and threw it out of me with intention. It was like a fountain of light bursting over me. Ysobi uttered a cry. I felt him pulse inside me, expelling his own flood. It was very hot. When his ouana-tongue pulled out from the fifth centre, I experienced another heady release, and this time, I let it be mine, not the town's, or anyhar else's. Waves of feeling throbbed through me from the roots of my hair to my toenails. My body would not let him go until it was done. It held him as I had wanted to hold him: tightly. It let him go reluctantly, once the sensations had subsided.

Ysobi withdrew fastidiously and covered himself. His hair had come loose, but otherwise he appeared composed. I was just a shaking mass on the floor before him, like a jellyfish stranded on sand. He put a blanket over me, pressed on my knees to make me lie flat. I turned onto my side, shuddering.

'You see,' Ysobi said. 'That is aruna magic.'

Yes, it was. I ached. I wanted to weep and laugh. I felt as if a universe turned inside me. I was immense, bigger on the inside than on the outside.

Ysobi moved away, and presently returned, bringing me a glass of unsweetened apple juice. This I drank greedily. The taste of it was intense; the very essence of apple.

'The soume har is the conductor in this type of work,' Ysobi said. 'It is his responsibility to build the power, contain it and release it. You did quite well for your first attempt. Well done.'

I couldn't speak, because all the things I wanted to say were inappropriate, such as how wonderful it had been, how amazing he was, how I wanted to hold him, share breath, and lie with him among the cushions until we fell asleep. Nohar had ever touched me that deeply, in any sense. He had no idea. To him, it was just work. I was bereft.

'You can take a bath before you leave, if you like,' he said.

I didn't want to. I wanted to keep the scent of him on me until it wore off on its own. Somehow, I managed to sit up, the blanket around me. 'I feel shaky,' I said, and realised that my teeth were in fact chattering.

'You should really take a warm bath, and perhaps you should sleep. It will be all right if you do that for a while. I have things I can get on with.'

How could he not be affected by what had just happened? It shocked me. I was so naïve, and he had proved it to me.

I dozed for a while, drifting in and out of sleep. I could hear Ysobi writing, the scratch of a pen on paper. Was he writing about me, a report of our experience? Eventually, he shook me to full wakefulness and gave me a cup of cinnamon tea. 'How do you feel?'

'Fine,' I lied. 'I've never experienced anything like that. It knocked me around a bit.'

'It can do that,' Ysobi said. 'It's very different when you take aruna for a purpose.'

To me, the purpose was irrelevant. *He* had done or shown those things to me. I wished he could have done it because he wanted me. I wished it hadn't been work.

'We'll work this way for a while, and soon it won't be so disorientating. You'll learn how to control it better.'

This news cheered me greatly. We would be together this way again. I felt better already.

I walked back to my cottage in a dream. I felt like dancing, yet was almost too tired to move. When I got home, I went and lay on my bed, face down. No way could I face going to the vineyard. My mind was numb. I didn't know what to think.

Minnow came knocking at the door later, so I had to get up and let him in. 'You look awful!' he said, as I led him into the kitchen: the social heart of my house. 'What's happened?'

'The arunic arts have happened,' I said, rubbing at my hair.

Minnow laughed. 'Ah! So you have sampled the famous mind-melting session.'

That was like a knife cut to my heart. 'Ysobi is known for it, then?'

Minnow nodded and sat down at my table. 'Pretty much, yes. Some hara find it too much to cope with. They don't like it. They think it makes aruna too clinical. He doesn't care. If the students can't cope and leave, it's no loss to him, or so he thinks. Will he lose you?'

I turned away to put some water on the stove to boil. 'No.'

'He's weird, I know.'

I concentrated on making a hot drink, because I didn't want Minnow to see my face. 'Does he ever go out?' I asked casually. 'I mean, have a social life.'

'Not really. He thinks the whole drinking and chatting thing is shallow, no doubt. He lives for his work.'

These comments stung me deeply. I hated the thought of Ysobi doing what he'd done to me to hundreds of others. It meant I meant nothing to him.

Why I should care about this mystified me, since he was only my teacher. Clearly, I needed to pull myself together.

'Are you OK to go out?' Minnow asked.

I thought I needed to. 'Yes,' I said. 'I want a drink... well, several.'

Minnow stood up and slapped me on the shoulder. 'Come back down to earth. Forget tea. Take the water off the stove. Let's go and find alcohol.'

It might have been drink that impelled me to do what I did that night, or simply a desire to get Ysobi out of my head. Whatever the reason, once we got to Willow Pool Garden, where Vole was waiting for us, I proceeded to drink to excess. The thunder had come and gone while I'd been asleep at home, and now the evening was clear; fresh-scented and balmy. We sat in the garden behind the bar, which overlooked the river. Hara sprawled on the lawns that went down to the water's edge. One group was singing, playing hand drums. I felt strangely ecstatic, as if Ysobi was there with me, or would come into the garden and look at me. It was a feeling of anticipation. I couldn't stop thinking of him, replaying the afternoon's events in my head. But at the same time, I was able to converse and laugh, play the part.

Zehn came up to our group, as usual with a new har in tow. 'Hello Jassenah,' he said to me. It was our habit now to snipe at each other, much to our friends' amusement. That night, I couldn't be bothered. I turned away from him to talk to somehar else. He didn't like that. He didn't like being ignored.

I continued to drink and even shared breath with

some har; I can't remember who it was. At one point, I was left alone, and I was just sitting there, staring at the willows, looking for tree spirits, completely intoxicated. It was then that Zehn decided to take me on. He sat down in front of me, apparently having shed his companion.

'You really think a lot of yourself,' he said. 'You're not as perfect as you like to think, Jass. Who the hell do you think you are?'

'Excuse me?' I laughed in his face.

'It's pathetic the way you think you're so much better than everyhar else, it really is. It makes you look stupid. Hara notice, you know.'

I smirked at him. 'Your opinions are of no interest to me, Zehn. What's the matter? Can't you get your head round the fact there's one har in Jesith who doesn't fancy you?'

He made an angry sound, started to say something, then shut his mouth. He shook his head.

I stared at him, wondering what I was really looking at. I felt powerful, because I knew he wanted me to like him. I knew how he felt, that was the thing. And I think that was what made me say it. 'I'm going home now. Do you want to come with me?'

He glanced up at me, and his eyes were dark and wide. He looked bitter. 'What?'

'You heard. The offer's there. It's up to you.' I stood up.

He stared at the table. I shrugged and walked into the bar. I saw Minnow heading back towards the garden and managed to avoid him.

The little street at the front of the Pool was empty and quiet. I waited a few seconds before I started to walk home. I wanted to see whether Zehn would come after me, and if he did, it would tell me a lot.

He caught up with me when I was halfway home. I heard the running footsteps and laughed softly to myself. I stopped walking but didn't turn round.

'Jass...'

Another feeling came into me, a sort of vengefulness. I stood for a moment and let the silence expand, then wheeled round and grabbed hold of him. I pressed my mouth to his, exhaled deeply, sent my breath deep inside him. He went limp in my arms, but returned the kiss. I hadn't shared breath with Ysobi. I knew he wouldn't do that with his students. What would it feel like to touch him that way?

I was light-headed myself before I broke away from Zehn. He slumped against me, his heart beating so fast and so hard I could feel it through our clothes. 'God,' he said.

I put his left hand through my right elbow and led him home.

Once we were inside the cottage, I thought about whether I wanted Zehn in my bed, or whether I should just push him onto the carpet. If I took him upstairs, it would probably mean he'd want to sleep here. 'Do you want a drink?' I asked him.

'OK.'

'Sit down,' I said.

He sat on my moth-eaten old sofa, which despite appearances was very comfortable. I gave him some wine. I always had wine, of course.

'Did you come here to Jesith to train?' I asked him.

He shook his head. 'No, I was incepted here, a

few years ago. A friend of Sinnar's brought me here.'
'Have you trained?'
'A bit. Is that all you're interested in?' He took a
drink. He was trembling.
'No, just curious.' I sat down beside him. He was a
different har now, unsure of himself, nervous. I took
the drink from his hand. 'We'll be friends. OK?'
He smiled at me rather bleakly. 'What's this about,
Jass?'
'You came here. You know what it's about.' I took
his face in my hands, bent my head to his. He knew I
wanted him to be soume and became so willingly. As
we shared breath, I put my hand between his legs and
stroked him through his trousers. I kept stroking him
gently until the cloth felt damp. Then I pulled away
from his mouth. He gasped, his eyes closed. I took off
his clothes, as Ysobi had done to me. I pushed him
back into the dusty cushions and raised his knees. His
soume-lam was a dark flower in the dim light, as were
the bunched folds of his ouana-lim, which had shrunk
into his body. I stared at him, wanting him to feel
vulnerable and exposed. I put a finger into him, felt for
the first energy centre and gently rubbed it. He
groaned and warmth spread over my hand. Then I
knelt before him on the floor and kissed the outer folds
of his soume-lam. He smelled fragrant, like violets. I
would do to him what I wanted done to me. When I
finally put my tongue inside him, the first sikra was
already a hard little nut. He put his hands on my head,
pulled me closer, raising his legs. Fluid gushed over my
face, he was so aroused. I drank it, feeling my ouana-
lim pressing painfully against my trousers. Reaching
down with one hand, I released it. I pushed my

trousers down to my thighs. I meant to do what Ysobi had done, just connect us hip to hip, but ultimately I couldn't do that.

I pushed Zehn round until he was lying on the sofa, then lay on top of him. When I pressed against him, I was at exactly the right angle and slid right inside him. He put his legs round my waist and we shared breath again. My face was wet against his. He licked me. I kept it slow and deep, ceasing movement when I sensed him begin to peak. He uttered soft little groans of pleasure, holding me close. We melted into each other: I was a hawk flying, a silver fish at the bottom of the willow pool. Beautiful visions cascaded through my mind. This was how it should be. I felt my own peak approaching, the tingle in my ouana-lim that presaged the darting tongue. Our movements became frantic, fluids foaming between us like horse's sweat. We were two sea creatures, bubbles all around us in the dark, writhing and pulsing. The ouana-tongue shot out and embedded itself. Aren jetted out around it; I could feel every pulse. Zehn pushed his legs high into the air and yelled. I felt the contractions, not just in his soume-lam, but throughout his whole body. In my mind, we shot out of our watery bed and took to the air, fins turning to wings. When the tongue came out of him, I began moving again, so he'd reach another peak. It was entirely physical then, like it had been for me with Ysobi. Zehn's cries were like those of pain. Then I lay still and heavy upon him.

For some minutes, neither of us spoke or moved, then Zehn began stroking my back. 'Jass,' he murmured. 'God, Jass.'

I raised myself and looked down at him. His lips

were heavy, almost bruised-looking, and his eyes were half closed. He looked sated, utterly sated. 'Now you know,' I said. 'Was it good?'

He laughed weakly. 'Good? Jass, that was... It was the sort of aruna I imagine chesnari would have, the sort you dream of, and always try to find.'

'You've done quite a lot of looking, haven't you?' I smiled. I didn't want that to be a spiteful question.

He nodded. 'Yes. My instincts were right, though. I knew there was something different about you.'

'I wanted to give you pleasure, that's all.' I got up from the sofa, and now he lay there with his legs open, totally unembarrassed. There would be stains left behind him. I handed him his drink again.

He would be confused, thinking that was the most wonderful aruna he'd ever had, and did it mean nothing to me?

'Why now?' he asked me. 'What was all that bitching about these last few weeks?'

'I don't like to be taken for granted,' I said. 'I thought it might be more interesting to make you work for me.'

'Have you ever been chesna with somehar, Jass?'

I stared at him steadily. 'No. I'm not looking for that.'

He looked away from me, sat up and reached for his clothes. If I were ever to be intimate with him again, it wouldn't be for a while. I felt contrite though, because he looked as if I'd punched him in the gut. Again, I knew that feeling.

'Hey, we're friends,' I said softly. 'Friends take aruna. Don't go weird on me. This is not the Zehn I know.'

'You've no idea,' he said, pulling on his shirt. 'You don't know me at all. You don't know how I feel.'

It occurred to me that I did. I went to him, held him close. 'It was good,' I murmured into his hair. 'Don't let it be spoiled.'

He laid his head on my shoulder and sighed. 'You want me to go now, right?'

I did, but relented. 'I was going to make myself something to eat. I've drunk too much. Are you hungry?'

'A bit.' He laughed; a watery sound, full of unshed tears. 'I never thought this would happen to me,' he said.

The following day, I was nervous about going to the Nayati. I was almost scared of facing Ysobi, sure that my face would betray me. When I knocked and entered his room, he was standing on a stool, watering some plants on a high shelf. 'Hi, Jass,' he said. 'Get yourself a drink. I won't be long.'

I went into his kitchen, noticing all the little details of his life: a plate left unwashed beside the sink, a note to himself left on the counter. When I went back into the main room, he was sitting on the floor. 'I think we should take things easy today. We'll look into some history. It's quite interesting to see the ways humans viewed arts such as ours.'

'All our arts?' I enquired.

'Yes. All of them.'

I sat down in front of him. 'I tried out some of your techniques on Zehn last night.'

Ysobi laughed. 'Well, you're commended for doing homework, but he's hardly a har I'd choose for such work. What were your results?'

'Nothing much. I just made him fall in love with me.'

Ysobi didn't laugh at that. 'Be careful,' he said. 'I think you're very responsive, and one day could be a hienama of arunic arts. It gives you power, and that's a responsibility. When you can do certain things to a har, take him to places inside himself he's never visited, it can be misinterpreted. It shouldn't be used to play with hara's feelings.'

'Believe me, I know that.'

Ysobi frowned. 'Is there something wrong, Jass?'

I shook my head. 'No. I'm just astounded how little I knew before. Have any of your students ever fallen in love with you, Ysobi?'

'I make it clear they shouldn't,' he said.

From then on, I had to act. Ysobi interspersed ordinary lessons with further teachings of his art, times to which I looked forward with joy and dread. I was always soume, and I wondered if there would ever come a time when he'd teach me the other role. I had to prevent myself from hanging on to him, pulling him into my arms when we'd finished or, worst of all, uttering some embarrassing endearments. As the weeks progressed, I fell for him more and more, an endless fall into a black pit. I loved everything about him: his humour, the way his face moved, his voice. I'd thought him strange-looking to start with, but his appearance had grown on me so much he was now the most beautiful har I'd ever met. He taught me how to store arunic energy for later use. He taught me how to control my body, but not how to control my heart.

As for Zehn, he was a casualty of Ysobi's effect on me. Superficially, we maintained a bantering friendship, but I could sense his pain. He had resolved to stifle his feelings, and it was a terrible fight for him. In some ways, it was good for him, because I knew he'd used many other hara, with little regard for their feelings. I hoped that now he would take more care, and understand the fragility of the harish heart. I couldn't be so cruel as to initiate anything between us again. It would only make things worse.

It was the gossip of Jesith that something had happened between Zehn and me. Minnow was delighted and pressed for details I would not give. Vole only gave me a sorrowful glance. 'Zehn is hurt,' he said. 'I know he has his ways, but he's a good har, really. Everyhar likes him.'

Other hara were amused by the fact that Zehn had met his match. This included a good percentage of the broken hearts he'd left in his wake. The redhead he'd been with when I'd first arrived, Fahn, said to me, 'It's about time he had some of his own medicine, Jass. You did the right thing. You were the only one who could. It wasn't as if he was just a free spirit; he wanted hara to adore him. He'd make you feel that way, then he'd walk away from you. I still think of him.'

I didn't want to hear these disclosures, even though I liked Fahn and we were becoming good friends. Zehn, it appeared, was no longer a free spirit, although you'd never have guessed that to look at him. I didn't notice any discernible change in his behaviour, but I congratulated myself on the fact I might have taught him something.

Summer was fading, and Sinnar's hara applied themselves to the harvest. There was so much to gather that often I worked late into the night. An air of celebration filled Jesith, building up to the great festival of Shadetide, the onset of winter.

My training was still progressing well, and I sensed a connection between Ysobi and myself that went beyond mere teaching. Was I imagining it? Sometimes, he looked at me in a certain kind of way, and I couldn't help wondering, but despite this there was also a barrier that stopped me overtly flirting or saying anything obvious. When we practiced arunic arts, he was still academic about the whole thing. I couldn't make up my mind whether he liked me or not, and there was no way I could discuss it with anyhar else. I felt sure my friends would somehow disapprove. Having a crush on my teacher seemed embarrassing and juvenile.

I had only one clue to go on, which gave me hope. One time, at the height of aruna, he said my name. It was like he said it to himself, not to me. His eyes were closed. I said his name too. He opened his eyes and looked at me, and I sensed I should have kept silent. He dismissed me early that day. I think he was furious with himself, but that had to be a good sign, didn't it?

Every night, before I slept, I fantasised about him. My dreams were not of aruna, but of conversations, meaningful ones. I invented a thousand different ways for him to tell me he loved me. In these fond imaginings, I was always in charge of the conversation. I said clever things, and occasionally made him weep. It was a pathetic exercise.

Still, my feelings weren't going to go away, and I
realised finally that if I didn't act in some way, I might
go mad or say something really regrettable.

One afternoon, as I prepared to leave Ysobi's
room, I said to him, 'Do you never go out, Yzzi?' By
this time, I felt it was safe to call him that.

'What?' He frowned. 'What do you mean?'

'I mean that you spend all your time working,
meditating, and so on. I think it would do you good to
let your hair down once in a while, if only slightly.
Why don't you come for a meal tonight at The
Leaping Cat? The food is the best there.'

He grinned. 'Are you offering me an invitation to
dinner?'

'Yes. Well?' I think my heart actually stopped
beating for a couple of seconds.

He narrowed his eyes, although he was still
smiling. 'I don't usually socialise with students.'

I laughed in what I hoped was a convincingly
carefree manner. 'Oh, really, Yz! It's a meal. I like
your company. Is that so bad?'

He considered for a moment, then said, 'Oh, all
right. Why not? What time?'

I thought I must have acted extremely well over
the past months. 'Come by my place around 7.30.'

'OK... Where do you live again?'

I told him.

When I left the Nayati, I could barely believe he'd
agreed to meet me. Was there a sign to be read in
this? He didn't socialise with students. That meant he
saw me as different.

When he turned up at my house, he looked different.

Gone was the robe. He was dressed in a dark shirt of soft linen and leather trousers. His hair looked clean, flowing over his breast. The sight of him melted me. 'Well,' I said in an ironic tone. 'Clearly this is an occasion for you.'

He laughed. 'You were right. I should be more in touch with the community. Thanks for asking me to come.'

'My treat,' I said. 'I've been doing a lot of overtime, so I can afford it.'

And it all went very well. We arrived at the Cat early, so we could get a good table, with a view of the street. I ordered everything he said he liked. We gossiped about other hara in the town. We laughed.

Around nine o'clock, a group of my friends came in and among them was Zehn. He came over to our table, and pulled a face at me behind Ysobi's back as if to indicate: *what the hell is he doing here?* 'There's a band from the Shadowvales playing at the Pool tonight,' he said. 'Everyhar's going.'

'I heard,' I said.

'We'll save you a place. Come over when you've finished your meal. It'll be packed. A lot of out-towners will show up.'

I screwed up my nose. 'Well, I'm kind of busy tonight.'

Zehn's eyebrows went up. 'Busy?'

'I'm spending the evening with a friend.'

Zehn frowned quizzically. 'Who? Can't they come too?'

I turned to Ysobi. 'We could go over, if you'd like to.'

Ysobi raised his hands, shrugged. He looked

cautious. 'I...'

Zehn laughed loudly. 'No! I don't believe it! Don't tell me you're out on a purely social level, Yz.'

I had never seen Ysobi look embarrassed, and the sight of it made me angry at Zehn. 'Yz and I are spending the evening together,' I said. 'We might come over later. We'll see how we feel. OK?' I bared my teeth at him in a fierce smile.

Zehn stared at me for a moment. He wasn't laughing now. 'Fine,' he said. 'See you.'

After he'd gone, Ysobi scratched at his hair and rubbed his face with both hands. He kept his fingers over his nose for a moment, eyes closed.

'Don't mind him,' I said. 'He lacks manners.'

Ysobi shook his head, reached for his glass. 'It's OK.'

'No, really. Zehn is jealous, that's all.'

'What of, Jass?' Ysobi drained his glass.

I didn't say anything.

'Look,' Ysobi said, 'maybe we shouldn't be doing this.'

'Why not?'

'I make it a principle not to socialise with my students, you know that. I hope you also know why.'

I folded my arms on the table top. 'Perhaps you should tell me.'

'Because of the nature of my work. Jass, I...' He rubbed his face again. 'Look, I can't get into relationships easily. It would be difficult for any har I'm with. My work is intense sometimes, you know that. Hara find that... problematical. I have to be there for my students, always, and that would often be at the expense of anyhar who shared my life.'

41

'I understand,' I said, and added casually, 'Yz, we're only having dinner. It's not a blood bond, or anything! Lighten up.'

'I've been burned,' he said. 'In the past.'

'I can see that. Stop worrying about it. We were having fun. Let's just erase the last few minutes and remember where we were.'

'Yeah.' Ysobi sighed. 'You remember you asked me a while ago if any student had ever fallen for me? You must know the answer. I have to be so careful.'

I ducked my head. 'I know.'

'It's different with you because you're older. More sensible, I guess.'

I put my head to one side, smiled in what I hoped was an understanding way. 'I like you, Yz. You've taught me so much. I won't do anything that will make you feel compromised or uncomfortable. I mean that. When the training is over, I want us to be friends. You should have friends. There's more to life than work.'

He refilled his glass from the jug of cider we'd ordered. 'You think you'll stay here in Jesith, then?'

'I haven't got anywhere better to go. I've put down roots now. I have a job, friends... I like it here.'

He nodded. 'It's a good place.'

There was a silence, then I asked: 'Do you want to go to the Pool?'

Ysobi hesitated. 'Why not? Let's get the tongues wagging. I've not been out to a bar for years, never mind watched live music.'

'Excellent!'

'Jass...' He drew in his breath. 'This *is* just a meal and a drink between friends, isn't it?'

I didn't answer immediately. Eventually, I said,

'You call the shots, Yz. If that's all you want, that's all it is.'

He laughed uncertainly. 'I can't give you anything.'

'I disagree. You can give quite a lot; good companionship, friendship. That shouldn't be a sacrifice. You're allowed to have a life.'

He reached out and touched one of my hands. 'Thank you.'

I meant what I said. If more came of it, I would naturally be overjoyed, but I was happy to take what he felt he could give. If that was the occasional meal together, I'd be grateful. It was more than most hara could get from him, I knew that.

As Ysobi predicted, our arrival together at Willow Pool Garden caused a stir. He knew just about everyhar there, of course, but not in this way. They were curious as to how I'd persuaded him to leave his Nayati. Still, on the whole, it seemed to me that hara were glad he was there. They berated him for not having joined them before.

The band was very good; they played fiddles and drums and flutes. They had dancers with them, who performed nearly naked, twining between members of the audience. Hara showered them with gifts. Inevitably, Zehn ended up with one of them by the end of the evening. Everyhar had drunk a lot, the mood was high. We piled out into the street around four in the morning, everyhar singing and horsing around. Ysobi put his arm round my waist. I had never seen him so happy. 'You enjoyed yourself, admit it,' I said.

He squeezed me a little. 'It's been fun.'

'Do you want a final drink before bedtime?'

'I could fit one more in,' he said.

'Come back to mine, then,' I said. 'Sample my staff privileges.'

'Sounds good.'

In my living room, I lit candles, noticing there was still a mark on the sofa where Zehn had lain. I threw a cushion over it. 'Sit down,' I said to Ysobi. 'I'll just go and peruse my 'cellar', see what I can find.'

He threw himself down on the sofa, and I padded out to the kitchen, where there was a cold room. Here I kept all the bottles that Sinnar had given me; he insisted all his hara took their pick of everything we made. I didn't feel too drunk, just nicely mellow. I chose a birch sap wine. It was one of the best.

The kitchen was in darkness. When I turned round to go back into it, Ysobi was standing behind me. I jumped in alarm. 'Yz! You spooked me.'

He took the bottle from my hand, put it on the table behind him. He took my forearms in his hands.

'Yz, what...?'

He put a finger to my lips. 'Ssh.'

Then we were sharing breath. He was so hungry for it. Drowning. I could feel his grief, his loneliness. What could I do but give of myself? *Drink*, I told him. *Drink all you want.*

We staggered against the table and knocked the bottle over. It smashed on the floor. Ysobi was hanging onto me so tightly I thought I'd black out. Then he broke away from me, pressed his forehead to my own. 'I'm sorry,' he said. 'You don't know how much.' He took a step back. 'I can't do this, and yet I had to. I can't do this to you.'

He fled.

I just stood there stunned for several minutes. Then, like an automaton, I began to clear up the smashed glass and the lake of splintery wine. There were tears on my face, yet I wasn't weeping.

I took another bottle from the cold room and opened it. Then I went into the living room and sat on the sofa, swigging from the bottle. What had happened? My mind was on fire. I'd felt his need. I'd experienced his feelings. He'd run away. I wouldn't usually see him for two days, since tonight was the beginning of the weekend. In two days, I had to formulate a script we could both live with.

Minnow came round at mid-day, but I ignored his knocking. I'd hardly had any sleep and the last thing I wanted was my friend's eager questions about the previous evening. When I was sure he'd gone, I got out of bed and dressed myself. I went into the kitchen and drank some water. Then I went to the Nayati.

There was no response to my knock, so I just tried the door and it was open. Ysobi's living room was empty. I called his name. Nothing. I went into the garden and found him there, cross-legged on the grass, deep in trance. I sat down opposite him, studying his face. He looked wretched. I know he became aware of my presence, I could just feel it, although he did not open his eyes.

'Yz, look at me,' I said.

His brow furrowed.

'I think you should talk to me. I'm not angry or needy. I'm concerned for you.'

He looked at me then. 'I shouldn't have done what I did. I saw in your breath...' He shook his head. 'I told you, I can't give you anything.'

'I think you should let me be the judge of that.'

'Jass, you *know*. There will be other students. There are always students.' He put his head in his hands. 'Last night, I saw the potential. It was like a beautiful garden, glimpsed through a half-open gate. I wanted to fall back into you, be safe with you. I wanted to talk with you over breakfast. I wanted to walk with you in the evening. And that is so, so dangerous.'

I went to his side. 'Why, Yz? Why is it dangerous? Do you think I'll be jealous of your students, cause trouble for you?'

He nodded. 'You don't know what it's like.'

'I'm willing to risk it,' I said. 'I want to.'

'I want to as well.' He took me in his arms then, and we shared breath for a long time. This was what I'd longed for so much. I couldn't help but shed a few tears. He kissed them away, stroked my face. 'Last night... Jass, I knew. I knew it wasn't just a meal between friends. I have tried to hide it so well, and so have you. How could we have lied to each other so cleverly? I love you.'

I had never imagined it would happen so simply and spontaneously: him saying those words I had longed to hear.

'Don't be afraid,' I said. 'Just don't. We'll live for the moment and see where it takes us.'

He nodded. 'I want to believe in the dream, Jass. I really do.'

I drew away from him. 'Come over later. I've got a

few things to do today. Then we can talk.'

'I will.' He kissed my cheek. 'Thanks for coming here. I told myself that if you didn't come, I must forget about it, but you had the courage to come.'

One thing I was sure of was that Ysobi had been very badly hurt in the past. He was afraid of being close to me, because he thought I'd eventually turn on him. I'd felt that in his breath. I think maybe it had happened to him more than once.

Back home, I tidied the house in a kind of euphoric delirium, then went out and fetched a few things from the market. Minnow turned up again in the afternoon, just when I got back, so I couldn't avoid him.

'Well?' he demanded.

'What is it?'

He folded his arms. 'You know what! You and Ysobi. Is it true?'

Insouciantly, I moved things around on the kitchen table. 'He didn't stay here last night, if that's what you mean. We went out together. That does not constitute a chesna bond.'

'Yz does not go out with anyhar,' Minnow insisted. 'Not now.'

I sensed he wanted to tell me something, but I didn't really want to hear it. Not from him. 'I know about that,' I said. 'We're friends, that's all. If it's meant to go any further, then it will. I have no expectations.'

'Don't get messed up,' Minnow said. 'Please, Jass. Be careful. Lots of hara have been taken under his spell while they train with him. It's a hazard.'

'I'm old and wise enough to look after myself,' I

said. 'I'm not stupid.'

Minnow's expression was dark. 'I know. But sometimes Ysobi *is*.'

'You said yourself, he doesn't see anyhar. This is different.'

Minnow shook his head and sighed. 'I hope so.'

Ysobi came round about 7.30 again. Like the previous night, he was not wearing his hienama gear. I made us dinner and we talked. Well, he talked mainly. There were no names mentioned specifically, and he skirted the subject, but I knew he was trying to tell me of failed chesna bonds before. He wanted me to assure him I wasn't going to take offence too easily. 'I'll be taking other students in the New Year,' he said. 'Maybe that will be the test.'

'I'm willing to take it,' I said. 'Really, Yz, don't worry. This is all too new. There's no point fretting about the future. It might never happen.'

'You're right. That's what I'd tell anyhar else.' He laughed. 'It's sometimes hard to practice what you preach.'

Now that I felt I had him, it was a delicious torment to keep my hands off him. I knew he wouldn't be leaving me that night. We went for a walk, as he'd dreamed of doing, holding hands in the darkness like harlings. We kissed briefly beneath the horse chestnuts that were shedding their glossy conkers. The air was chill, smelling of smoke and ripe fruit. We stroked the friendly sheep in the field next to my cottage, who came to us like ghosts over the grass, seeking the titbits I'd often give them. Then we went inside again.

'Do you want a hot drink?' I asked him.

'Please,' he said. 'Bring it upstairs.'

'OK.'

He smiled at me and headed for the stairs.

When I went up, he was lying in my bed, his dark hair spread out around him. I couldn't believe this was happening. It was literally a dream come true. I gave him the drink and he sat up to sip it. I sat beside him on top of the covers and kissed his bare shoulders. The room was warm because I'd built a fire in there earlier. There was no way I wanted to be inhibited by huddling beneath the blankets in a freezing room.

'I'm nervous,' Ysobi said. 'Can you believe it?'

I stroked his back. 'Yes. This will be different. We both know that.'

He grimaced. 'You'll see inside me. I hope you like what you see.'

'Hush.'

He put down the mug on the bedside table and lay back, staring up at me. His expression was almost pleading. I stood up and took off my clothes, then climbed in beside him. In the light of my dim bedroom oil lamp, he looked like the most exotic har ever to walk the earth. I held him close, shared breath with him. For a time, we lingered in the outer courtyard of pleasure; the stroking of sensitive skin, the caress of silky hair, the light kisses on neck and arms. Then his fingers closed around my ouana-lim and gently massaged me. I reached down and put my hand over his ouana-lim, felt it slowly draw back into him, like a soft fragile creature retreating into a cave. He opened his legs for me, all the time staring into my eyes. I wanted to taste him, as he had tasted me so many times, but perhaps not now. I caressed his soume-lam a little, very gently. He was swollen with desire, slippery beneath my fingers. He pulled me onto him and I entered him carefully, with reverence. I felt him seize me, the folds clenching around me. We moved together in the simple act of aruna and he opened his mind to me. It was elemental, the fusing of waves and fire, but the waters were serene and the flames were an eternal pure blue. I had never been with a har like this, so full of love. Our union felt like the ultimate privilege bestowed upon hara by creation. It was such a gentle thing. When we reached our climax, it was like the river flowing, caressed by willow branches, cool and clean. He said my name, held me close. It was like coming home, after a long time away.

2

There is a particular kind of har who might as well have been incepted from a spiteful teenage human female. Back north, a friend of mine used to call them 'soume shrews'. The phenomenon is mostly encountered, we observed, in hara incepted quite young, i.e. below sixteen years. It is also seen in some second generation hara, perhaps being a stage that they have to go through after feybraiha, as they get to grips with the different aspects of their blossoming sexuality. The attributes of the condition are always the same: a particularly soume kind of beauty, of which they are totally aware; a desire to manipulate others through the power of their allure; a tendency to vengeful grudges; disregard for the feelings of others; a helpless attraction to hara in established chesna bonds that they seek to destroy; an ability to become simpering and vulnerable at will (usually used in devastating conjunction with the previously mentioned trait); and finally, a core of tempered steel. I'm sure you see the picture I'm painting here. You've no doubt met these types yourself. And I'm equally sure you can imagine what's coming next. I'm talking about a har called Gesaril, who came to Jesith two weeks after the winter solstice to train with Ysobi.

For a couple of glorious months after Ysobi and I got together, I lived in bliss. Ysobi did not move in with me, but we saw a lot of each other and spent the night together around three or four times a week. We socialised a lot, glowed radiantly, and became known as the epitome of what a perfect chesna bond could be like. The only har who didn't share in our happiness, of course, was Zehn, but even he was gracious enough to maintain the appearance of carefree friendship in public. I knew that Ysobi would be taking on new students in the New Year, and we'd discussed it. I can't say I was overly delighted to think of him in intimate situations with these as yet unknown hara, but I'd worked hard at overcoming vestiges of human jealousy. Ysobi and I were in love. We were unassailable. I'd always known what his work entailed. I would be adult about it. If ever there was a case of somehar painting a large red circle on his forehead, giving a gun to his worst enemy and saying 'I bet you can't hit me,' I was it.

My training for now had slowed down. Ysobi had taken me to Acantha, first level Ulani, and we planned to wait awhile before I progressed to Pyralis. He had a couple of other students lined up, and had told me that sometimes he would have a bunch of hara to train together, then there'd be a few weeks' or months' lull, when he'd take a rest. It had been unusual I'd been his only student during my training.

We spent the winter solstice festival, Natalia, with Sinnar and his family. They lived in a large house set into a hillside a mile or so from the vineyard. Sinnar had a chesnari himself and a young harling, which he'd hosted. That had meant his chesnari, Tibar, had had to run the vineyard for a couple of months, earlier in the year. Tibar came from the Shadowvales. I'd not really seen the harling close up before, even though Tibar sometimes brought him to the yard, and found the little creature rather unsettling. In some ways, he didn't look or behave like a child, even though physically he was small. It seemed inconceivable to me that Sinnar had hosted him; had grown a pearl in his body, expelled it like a hen laying an egg. Altogether, the thought of the process made me feel somewhat nauseous. I knew that hara had to breed, because available humans for inception would eventually be a thing of the past, but the idea of chesnari cosily making harlings seemed too human for me, a flashback to an imaginary past.

When I got the chance, I told Ysobi quietly about my feelings, to see what he thought.

He only said, 'Harlings aren't that easy to make.'

Over dinner, Tibar revealed one of the reasons (I think) that we'd been invited to share their festival meal. A friend of Tibar's back in his hometown had a son who had passed feybraiha in the summer. He'd asked Tibar if the renowned Ysobi would train this son to Brynie level. Tibar wanted to ask Ysobi face to face, once Ysobi had had a bit to drink and was in a good mood. The reason for this cautious delay in making the request soon became apparent. Tibar was an honest har, and felt obliged to tell Ysobi that his friend had had trouble with his son. 'He desperately needs training, some self-discipline at least,' Tibar said. 'He'll be a handful, Yz. But we'll be paid generously, both Jesith and you yourself. What do you say?'

Tibar perhaps didn't know Ysobi as well as I thought I did, but he was aware that our hienama couldn't resist a challenge.

'OK,' said Ysobi.

In the early hours of the morning, we walked back to my house through the snow, arm in arm. The world was silent and still and magical. It had reclaimed itself and I felt glad for it. Wraeththu had ushered in a new age. These fond thoughts were kindled because I'd had a lot to drink; I felt nicely mellow. I reflected that I now had quite a high status in Jesith. As chesnari of the town's most prominent hienama, I was invited to functions at the phylarch's house. I knew Sinnar would promote me at work. I felt as if life couldn't get any better.

At home, Ysobi made us drinks, while I went up to bed. The room was very cold, because the fire had gone out hours ago, and I was eager to cocoon myself in blankets. When Ysobi came into the room, there was a look I didn't recognise in his eyes. It made me feel strangely excited yet full of trepidation. 'What are you thinking?' I asked him.

He shook his head. 'I don't know yet. I enjoyed today, didn't you?'

'Yes. Are you thinking about that har Tibar told you about?'

'No. Not at all.' He began to undress.

It was a show I would never tire of, he was so beautiful. When he was naked, he shook out his hair and my heart turned over. I noticed his ouana-lim was slightly erect.

When we took aruna together, we didn't often bother with all the pyrotechnics of Ysobi's considerable skills. We found pleasure and contentment in a fairly basic union, when we'd mingle our thoughts and our dreams. He aroused me so much, I could reach a peak just by having him press against me for a few minutes. And the peaks were, for me, an energy expression of my intense love for him. I could often see the light of them.

That night, after he'd shaken out his hair, he brushed it back with his fingers and then wound it into a long rope, which he knotted at the nape of his neck. I knew what that meant. He got into bed and shared breath with me for a few moments. He felt different, somehow driven and sure about something. Presently, he began to kiss my chest and stomach, before burrowing down the bed to the cave my raised knees had made in the blankets. As he tongued me, I had the feeling this was all for a reason. It was like the training again, precise and measured. For some reason, this aroused me more. He spent some time tantalising my third sikra, then began to use his fingers on me. He pinched the nubs of the sikras till they hurt, but it was a hurt I craved. He went deep inside me, opening me up, reaching for the higher sikras. He was breathing very heavily.

'Yz,' I murmured. 'What is it you want to do?'

He didn't say anything. After what seemed like hours of agonising delight, when he'd manipulated me to the point of release several times without satisfying me, he finally lay upon me. I felt the petals on the head of his ouana-lim pressing against me, hard as wood. He rubbed the first sikra for a while, then progressed to the second. I was becoming lost in an ocean of insane visions, which were like opium dreams. The waves of sensation in my body were like waves of sound. I could also smell them. I could see a row of stars before me, exploding suns, which I knew were sikras. They pulsed with different colours. There were five of them, but if I directed my attention slightly to the side of them, it seemed there were another two, very faint, above them. And above them was a golden egg of light. It made me think of a dehar, some supernatural being.

Inside my body, the sikras were like musical notes, or the strings of an instrument. I could feel Ysobi playing each one, making the music. For a moment, I was back completely in the physical. Ysobi was thrusting into me strongly, but his whole body was shaking. Something was happening inside me, something immense. It was more than climax. For a moment, I was afraid.

Then we were in the eye of the storm, and Ysobi was looking into my eyes. 'There are more than five sikras in the soume-lam,' he said matter-of-factly, which seemed absurd, as if he was back to teaching me. 'The other two are accessible only rarely, and for a special purpose.'

'What do you want to do?'

'I want a pearl with you, Jass. I've never done it. I had to see whether we were capable, and we are. I can feel it, can't you? The sixth sikra is about to open, and beyond it lies the seventh, the cauldron of creation. But if you want to stop now, we will. I'll end it in the usual way. Will you do this with me?'

I remembered, then, how I'd often caught him watching Sinnar and his son that day. I remembered how I'd felt about the harling, my distaste. And yet, here I was, swooning in waves of aruna's potent tides, and he asked me a question like that. My world at that time was comprised of the most glorious colours: I felt

I loved everything in it. Would it be so bad? I wondered. As a har, surely I should experience this essentially female aspect of my being? Sinnar and Tibar would help me, and I had Ysobi, who loved me. He had asked me to make what was, for me, a big sacrifice. He had never done it with anyhar before. I wanted to give him this thing, the ultimate expression of what I felt for him. Not least, because I could.

'Don't end it,' I said, and pulled his head down to kiss him.

We stayed that way, lip to lip, as he continued the process that would result in our son. The sensation was not entirely pleasant, because the tongue of his ouana-lim really had to dig deep into the flesh of the sixth sikra to open it up. It was like a barbed arrow, and I was virgin there. Then, it didn't hurt any more and the fever dreams swept over me again in a vast tsunami. I became nothing other than the cauldron of creation, the heart of the universe where stars are born. The seventh sikra, I found, was not in my body, but somewhere else, linked to me. I was filled with a scalding stream of stars, which I knew was Ysobi's aren: a sparkling mist, which was my yaloe, tumbled over them, enfolding them. Sparks shot out in every direction. A soul was knitted into the raw stuff of creation; the essences of our bodies.

We actually fell asleep, still joined, and I dreamed I walked with our harling in a meadow of yellow flowers. He introduced himself to me, said he was happy he would come to us. Perhaps it was just a dream.

The following morning, Ysobi and I hardly spoke to

one another, because what we'd experienced was beyond words. Also, I felt numb and shocked. We went for a long walk in the afternoon, and then in the evening to Minnow and Vole's house, since we'd been invited there for a party. My whole body was still thrumming with the aftershock of what had happened. I knew my eyes were alight.

Minnow noticed something different about me at once. 'You look really strange,' he said, taking the gifts from my hands that we'd brought for him and his brother. 'Not bad, but really strange. Are you all right?'

We were in the living room, which was lit by candlelight and warmed by an enormous fire that blazed in the hearth. The air smelled of cut evergreen and spiced wine. Around fifteen other hara were present. Others had yet to arrive. But Zehn was there. I almost didn't want to speak, but knew I had to. 'I've got some news,' I said.

Conversations died down. I don't know what they expected. Now, I didn't want to say anything.

Ysobi took over. 'Last night, we made a pearl.'

There were several moments of stunned silence, then Fahn came to us and embraced us both. He kissed our faces. 'You're blessed,' he said. 'You'll bring a wondrous new soul to Jesith.'

I was overcome with a strange kind of embarrassment. I wished Ysobi hadn't said anything. I couldn't look at Zehn; he was the only one who didn't come to embrace and congratulate us. What could I say to make him feel better? Nothing.

Later, once everyhar was playing music, dancing or singing, and the wine and ale were flowing,

Minnow drew me into the kitchen. 'I've got to hand it to you, Jass,' he said, 'you've done wonders with Ysobi. Nohar ever thought he'd go into a chesna bond again. You've revived him. I'm sorry I doubted you.'

'This will be weird for me,' I said.

'You *are* totally OK with it, aren't you?' Minnow looked concerned.

I answered too quickly. 'Yes, of course.' It was hard to meet his gaze. 'Well, it feels a bit strange, I don't deny it, but it feels kind of right too.'

'At least harlings grow up quickly,' Minnow said. 'Before you know it, he'll be har.'

'Hmm. I think I'll need all the help I can get, though. This wasn't exactly planned.'

'So how *does* it happen, then?' Minnow was always eager for intimate details.

'Hard to describe,' I replied. 'You can't do it with just anyhar. You have to be chesna, I think. It's a shattering experience. I haven't got over it yet.'

'I can tell. You look great, though.' Minnow sighed. 'It's a bit disorientating. I mean, I know Tibar and Sinnar have done it, but not many others here in Jesith. Some of us are beginning to take the plunge, obviously, really embracing what it means to be Wraeththu. It's brave of you, Jass. It really is. You were a human male once.'

'Shut *up!*' I said. 'I don't want to think about that. It makes me feel freakish.'

Minnow narrowed his eyes, observed me keenly. 'It was Ysobi's idea, wasn't it?'

I made a careless gesture with one hand. 'It was a mutual idea. We're celebrating. Let's get on with it.'

I spent the next week paying extra attention to my body, trying to discern changes within me. I felt little different to how I'd felt before, but I guessed this would change as the pearl developed. I had to keep telling myself there was life inside me, because it didn't feel real. The memory of creating it began to blur in my mind. Perhaps it hadn't really happened and we'd just thought we'd done it. Then I started to get twinges in my belly and when I pressed my flesh, it felt hard beneath. Something was growing there. At times, it made me panic and I thought it would be easy then to give in to insanity, to run outside screaming, tearing at my skin.

Eventually, I went to see Sinnar. I had to talk to somehar, and he was happy to oblige me. I don't think he'd ever harboured doubts and fears like mine.

'Anxiety is normal,' he said. 'It takes a while to get used to the idea, but it is a natural thing, Jass, so just let nature do its work.'

'How long will it take for the pearl to... form?' I wanted to know.

'Oh, between two and a half or three months,' he said. 'When it's ready, you'll drop it, and then it will take a couple more weeks for the harling to be ready to emerge from the pearl. Let me be with you for the drop. I won't lie to you: it's not the most edifying of experiences.'

'Hurts?'

He pulled a sour face. 'Have you ever been tortured?'

I winced. 'Fortunately, no.'

'Well, all I'll say is the worst torture cannot be as bad.' I must have looked horrified, because Sinnar smiled and gripped one of my hands. 'We'll do what we can for you to make it happen quickly. There are certain herbal drinks you can take beforehand to assist matters. There are things I can do, or show Ysobi how to do if you prefer, that help the soume-lam cope with it all.'

'Do you go back to normal afterwards?' I couldn't keep the horror from my voice, since it was now too late to change my mind.

Sinnar laughed. 'Completely! We're not human, Jass. Within a week, nohar will be able to tell you've ever carried a pearl. There are benefits to it, too, I noticed. I'm more sensitive to touch than I was before. Let's just say that Tibar is delighted with the changes.'

Ysobi seemed so pleased about the pearl, I hadn't the heart to discuss my fears with him. He felt it was an achievement, that it proved our chesna bond was not only right but superior. I think that to him we were like gods.

After a couple of weeks, my shock and horror began to subside, perhaps because chemicals in my body made it happen to ensure the pearl's survival. I still had to endure the curiosity of my friends, but life went more or less back to normal. I prepared myself daily for the arrival of the first student: Gesaril from Shadowvales. Another would be coming a couple of weeks after that. Then there was a gap until the Spring Equinox, when a third would arrive. At that point, it would be most likely Ysobi would have three to train at once, at varying levels of experience. I wouldn't let myself think about the implications too much, but I sensed our aruna life would suffer in the spring. However, at that time, I'd no doubt be occupied with the harling, who would have emerged from the pearl by then, or be just about to.

Zehn was doing some deliveries for Sinnar, and one afternoon, we bumped into each other in one of the must-rooms at the vineyard. There were some moments of awkwardness, then he said, 'I'm happy for you, Jass. I guess you found the thing I've always been looking for.'

I didn't know how to respond. I shrugged. 'I didn't expect it, Zehn. It just happened.'

Zehn laughed bleakly. 'It's that training he does, I guess. I heard about it. Is that what you used on me?'

I was horrified to realise my face had coloured up. 'Zehn…'

'It's OK,' he said, raising his hands. 'I don't regret it, nor will I ever forget it. I'd die for you, Jass. I want you to be happy. You can always call on me as a friend, if ever you need help.'

'Thanks.' I embraced him briefly, but he was unyielding in my hold.

Gesaril arrived one afternoon, but I didn't get to meet him straight away. Ysobi came over in the evening and informed me his new student was 'as exasperating as they come. Shall we say high maintenance?'

'Spoiled brat?' I enquired, pleased to hear it.

He laughed. 'Yeah, very much so. Note to self: do not indulge son too much!'

'Think you can train him?'

'Give me a whip and a chair, and there's a fair chance. He thinks it's all beneath him, but his parents are keen for him to have the labels of the levels, as it were. They're quite high-ranking, it's obvious.'

I imagined an obnoxious, cocky little har, who would no doubt be very much like the obnoxious, cocky little humans I'd hung out with before I was har. I'd probably been the same way myself. Perhaps I should be more understanding. 'He's young,' I said. 'Getting to know himself. Maybe it'll be all right.'

'Come here,' Ysobi said, and pulled me onto his lap. He put a hand on my belly, nuzzled my neck.

Things did not go well with the training. Ysobi would come to visit me and get the closest to ranting in anger that he was capable of. Gesaril was rude, inattentive and disruptive. When Ysobi tried to teach him a technique, even as basic as mind touch, he'd just say something like, 'Why the fuck should I?'

'So often, I long to throw him out,' Ysobi said to me.

'Then, why don't you?' I asked.

Ysobi only grimaced. 'I can't do that. The training's hardly begun. How would it appear to his hara at home?'

I really didn't care. I couldn't understand why Ysobi wanted to persist with a hopeless case. If he was worried about his reputation, he could always say that the har wasn't of high enough standard for him to teach. But Ysobi wouldn't give up. He was sure he could reach this har.

'He's behaving this way for a reason,' Ysobi said. 'He's bright, and could do the work easily. I want to get to the bottom of it.' He shook his head. 'He just won't let anyhar in.'

Somehow, I couldn't see the arunic arts figuring

greatly in Gesaril's education. That is, not until I met him.

Gesaril had been in Jesith for over a week. A couple of bands were in town, so Ysobi and I went out at the weekend to see them play. As usual, the event was at Willow Pool Garden, since it was the largest hostelry we had. We sat down with our friends, and were indulging in idle gossip, when I saw him. I didn't know who it was. I just saw this beautiful creature and remember thinking he had 'Zehn' written all over him. 'Yz,' I said discreetly. 'I think there's an out-towner here we could put money on, in terms of Zehn having him later on.' I jerked my head in the new har's direction.

Ysobi glanced over his shoulder. He sighed, rolled his eyes and said sarcastically, 'Oh, great.'

I knew then who it was.

The har in question sashayed over to our table. He had thick brown hair, cut to his shoulders and astounding straight black eyebrows, with sultry dark eyes beneath. His lips were full, made to kiss. 'Ysobi,' he said. 'I wouldn't have thought this was your kind of thing.' He glanced at me, summing me up in seconds.

'Gesaril,' Ysobi said wearily, 'this is my chesnari, Jassenah. Jass, this is my latest student.'

'Hi,' said Gesaril. One shoulder was bare, since the oversize, soft wool jumper he wore kept slipping off it. He spent a lot of time needlessly sliding it back, only for it to drip once more seductively to his elbow.

I nodded to him. My hackles were up. I knew his type. I was actually praying for Zehn to show up. Now that the charming Gesaril was aware his teacher had a chesnari, Ysobi would become infinitely more fascinating to him. I just knew it. And Gesaril was exquisite, in that mean, careless way his kind has. He was an ouana-charmer. Hara would fall helplessly and mindlessly before him.

'Are you enjoying your training?' I enquired pleasantly.

He wrinkled his perfect nose. 'It's OK. Yzzi insists it's all essential stuff, but I just want to get to the interesting part. I know what he's famous for!' He laughed beautifully, while I froze from the gut outwards. With these words, knowing how accurately he'd hit his target, no doubt, Gesaril sauntered off, with a languid wave of one hand and a drawled: 'See ya!'

Don't be ridiculous, I told myself. *He's a posturing fool. He's an empty pretty shell, that's all.* Then I could see him on the cushions in the Nayati, his gorgeous body spread out, his face transfigured by pleasure, those wonderful lips slightly open. I could see Ysobi's head between his legs, and I heard the moans he would make. I felt sick.

'Jass?' Ysobi said. He sounded worried.

I shook my head. 'What a little shit!'

'I know. I'll speak to him. He doesn't realise you're with pearl.'

I hadn't realised it was possible for my frozen innards to go colder. 'Don't tell him,' I said quickly.

Ysobi frowned. 'Why not? He's being flirty. He should know it's not really appropriate at the moment. Your emotions are up and down.'

I wanted to stand up and leave. I felt furious, not least because of Ysobi's rather patronising remark. 'He called you Yzzi,' I said. 'How come he's so familiar with you after so short a time?'

'He does it to try and wind me up,' Ysobi said. 'Ignore it. I do.'

I shook my head. 'He's trouble,' I said. 'Be careful, Yz.'

'I know he's trouble,' Ysobi said. 'I don't need you to tell me.' He squeezed my shoulder. 'Just enjoy yourself. Forget him.'

I did try. But all evening, I had to endure the butterfly presence of Gesaril, whose laughter reached far. He was forever messing with his hair, twisting little locks of it, chewing it, or else trying to pull his clothes back on. Always, wherever he was in the room, his glance kept sliding towards our table. He didn't care that I noticed.

Zehn arrived late, accompanied by a har called Arken, who was another fairly recent addition to our community, not yet shattered by Zehn. He was a good-natured and attractive har, fair-haired like Zehn, and very tanned. I hoped Zehn wouldn't damage him too much. I hoped he could find a companion in Arken, somehar to care for. Hara called them over to our group, and Zehn had little choice but to comply, even though I was aware he hated being near me, especially when Ysobi was there. I didn't want to make his evening miserable, and in fact was feeling quite tender towards him, mainly because of the vileness of Gesaril. At one point, we were sitting close to one another. I smiled at him and leaned towards him to say, 'Arken's lovely, Zehn. You look good together.'

He smiled back thinly. 'How are you?'

'Fine. Have you met Ysobi's new student?'

He shook his head.

'I'm tempted to ask you to do your stuff on him. He's a monster.'

Zehn laughed a little. 'When I said I'd always help you out, I didn't think you'd expect my services to extend that far.'

'I'm joking. I wouldn't wish him on anyhar.'

Gesaril had stopped by our table several times during the evening, clearly to display himself to Ysobi, who I'm glad to say didn't react. The next time he came by, he spotted Zehn, who in the beauty contest stakes could give the little horror a run for his money.

'You must be Zehn,' he said. 'I've heard about you.'

Zehn gave him a cold eye. 'Who are you?'

'Hasn't Yzzi's chesnari told you?' I had no doubt he remembered my name, just chose not to use it.

Zehn merely shook his head. He turned to me. 'I'm going to the bar. You want a drink, Jass?'

'Please. I'm trying to be good and not have too much.' I didn't want to say more.

'I understand. I'll get you something not too toxic.' Zehn stood up.

'I'm Gesaril,' the horror said, in a tone that implied he thought Zehn must surely know who he was.

'Congratulations,' Zehn said. He brushed past Gesaril. 'Excuse me.'

Gesaril was left standing there before me. I smiled sweetly, then looked the other way.

Of course, the only thing that this scenario amounted to was a declaration of war.

It didn't take long for Gesaril to change his tactics,

although he didn't put them into play until after the new student turned up. This was Orphie, a shy and fairly withdrawn young har, who was second generation as Gesaril was. I took a liking to Orphie straight away, perhaps for obvious reasons. In retrospect, I can see that I'd begun to burgeon with nurturing instincts, but Orphie was also such a welcome change from the other one. I asked Ysobi if he'd mind me asking Orphie to come and eat with us sometimes, and he said he had no objection. He'd become a lot more open, since me.

The first time Orphie came to my house, he could barely speak to me. He was a small, fragile creature, with soft light brown hair, a pointed elfin face and enormous doe-like dark eyes. It was hard to credit he'd been through feybraiha a year before. I tried to make him feel at ease, and got him to help me prepare the meal. When it was ready to eat, Ysobi hadn't arrived yet. It was not like him to be late. I opened some wine, and poured Orphie and me a glass each. The dinner was being kept warm on the stove. If Ysobi didn't come soon, it would spoil.

The atmosphere became ever more strained, until I said, 'Well, perhaps we should just eat.'

Orphie agreed at once; no doubt grateful the consumption of food mitigated the need for conversation.

We were halfway through the meal when Ysobi finally appeared. I didn't like the look of him. He was agitated. Without questioning him, I fetched his dinner. He played with it for a while. Eventually, even though Orphie was there, I had to ask: 'Is everything OK, Yz?'

He frowned. 'Yes. I'll talk to you later.'

Perhaps sensing his presence was awkward, Orphie fled almost as soon as we'd finished eating, which effectively ruined my plans of warm conversation to help him relax into Jesith's way of life. Ysobi took the dishes into the kitchen, and after a while I followed him.

'It's Gesaril, isn't it?' I said, standing at the threshold.

'It wasn't good,' Ysobi said, with his back to me.

'What wasn't?'

'We...' He put down a dish into the sink and turned round. 'Let's go back to the other room.'

My heart had stilled. I felt I had become partly dead.

In the living room, I sat on the sofa and stared at him. 'What do you want to tell me?'

Ysobi sat opposite me on a chair, leaned forward. 'He fell apart on me, Jass. I've never seen anything like it.'

I frowned. 'That doesn't mean anything to me. What happened? Have you begun the arunic arts?'

Ysobi nodded. 'This afternoon, yes.'

A chill skittered through me. I didn't want to hear more, and yet I knew I had to.

Ysobi sighed through his nose before speaking. 'At first, it was just as if he was uncomfortable with it, which happens. I kept it low key. It's an important phase, as you know. It helps a har to reach his potential. It's vital it goes smoothly. Anyway, I... Jass, I don't want to upset you... Can you cope with this?'

No, most likely not. I swallowed. 'We talked about this, Yz. I'm your chesnari. You can speak to me about anything.'

He closed his eyes briefly. 'Thanks. Anyway, we were reaching the end of it, when he started moaning. At first, I thought... Well, you can imagine. The peak came, and it seemed all right to me, then he screamed. He didn't stop screaming. He was hysterical. I pulled out of him and there was blood, quite a lot of it.'

'What?' I could see it in my mind's eye. I could smell it.

Ysobi had gone very pale. 'It must have been my fault. He's young, not long past feybraiha. I must have torn him. He was tight, Jass, and I know that because of all the arunic work I've done...' He gestured helplessly. 'It was like I'd butchered him. He must have been bleeding for some time, but I hadn't noticed.' He clenched his hands into fists. 'I should have noticed.'

'God.' I put my head in my hands. That was far too much detail. My stomach turned over. I could taste sour metallic wine in my throat.

'I had to calm him down, stay with him, give him healing. The bleeding stopped eventually.' Ysobi groaned in utter bewilderment. 'It's never happened to me before. I don't understand it. It wasn't as if I'd lost control. I was being careful. I...'

I couldn't bear any more. The stink of blood, the *taste* of it, consumed my senses. I stood up and went to the kitchen, where I vomited over the dirty dishes. I felt it would never end, or I'd throw up my insides. It was like I'd been poisoned. My belly ached. There were spots of light before my eyes.

Ysobi came in after me, leaned against my back, held my stomach. He made soothing noises, and when I'd finished retching said, 'I'm so sorry, Jass.'

'It's OK,' I managed to say. I turned on the tap and let water splash over my cupped hands. I drank as much as I could to get rid of that hideous taste. 'I'm just feeling queasy. I should stop drinking wine until after the pearl has dropped.'

Ysobi held me tighter. 'You don't want to hear these things, I know, and your body's in a state unknown to you. But you're the only one I can talk to.'

'I know. I'm all right with it, Yz, honestly, but it's still a shock to hear it.' I took another drink of water from the tap and turned round in Ysobi's arms to face him. Somehow, I was able to ask: 'How is he now?'

'I left him at my place. He's sleeping.' Ysobi paused. 'I think I'll have to go back tonight. He doesn't look good. It's like he's in shock.'

'Oh.'

He tilted my chin up with one hand. 'Jass, you *do* understand, don't you?'

'Yes,' I said, perhaps too sharply. 'You warned me. I stand by what I said.'

He kissed me, but I wanted to pull away. I guessed he'd had his mouth on Gesaril's soume-lam, and it felt contaminated.

It took every shred of will I possessed to calm myself about this situation. I didn't doubt that Gesaril had been hurt, but part of me wondered if he'd done something to himself to make it happen. He had Ysobi concerned for him, worried because he thought he'd caused injury. Effectively, he now had Ysobi's full attention and I couldn't believe that wasn't a strategy.

That night, I couldn't sleep properly. If I did manage to doze off, I would hear screaming and wake up, with echoes of a cry winging round my room. I felt feverish and was perhaps hallucinating. Was Ysobi holding Gesaril in his arms now? I don't know how I got through that night. I realised that my condition must be exacerbating my feelings and reactions, but I couldn't dispel a terrible feeling of dread.

Ysobi came to me early the next morning. Nohar locks their doors in Jesith, so he came right up to my bedroom, where I'd eventually drifted off into a troubled sleep. He sat on the bed and shook me awake. 'Hey,' he said softly. 'I'm going to make you breakfast. Don't get up.'

I yawned and pulled myself into a sitting position. 'How is he?' I asked coldly.

Ysobi stroked my hair. 'Better,' he said. 'He apologised, which astounded me. He really seems abashed about what happened, as if it was his fault, which I don't think it was at all.'

'And where is he now?' I snapped, unable to find the slightest shred of sympathy within me.

'He's gone back to his lodgings. He told me he was fine, and that I should come to you. I explained you were with pearl.'

My deep suspicions descended a further few miles towards the centre of the earth.

After that, I couldn't bring myself to ask Ysobi how the arunic training progressed, and he offered no further information. I made myself pretend it wasn't happening, that Gesaril wasn't using every wile he owned to manipulate my chesnari. But Ysobi spent more and more time with Gesaril, ostensibly because he needed support. For somehar who was so fragile and damageable in the soume department, I thought, he seemed to want to spend a lot of time having it stretched to capacity. I was obsessive, and at that time forgot that caste training includes a lot more than arunic arts. I was in such a state I felt that Ysobi was taking aruna with Gesaril continually. I spoke to nohar about the situation, and maintained a cheerful front.

Occasionally, we'd run into Gesaril when we were socialising. He was always civil to me in front of Ysobi, but wasn't quite the same on the rare occasions we met and Ysobi wasn't there. Once, I had to walk past him on the way back from the bathroom in the Pool, and he decided he wanted some sport. He caught hold of my arm and said, 'How are you, Jassenah?'

'Fine.' I smiled politely and made to move away from him.

But he wouldn't let me go. 'It must be really weird having a pearl inside you. I don't think I'd like it. It's like a parasite sapping all your strength.' I assumed that was a way to tell me I wasn't looking my best.

'Actually, it feels good,' I said, finally shaking off his hold. 'When you're old enough, you should try it.'

He laughed. 'I don't think I'll ever be old enough. I know hara have to do it, but I wouldn't want to have my life taken over in that way. I like having fun too much.'

'Well, maybe you'll feel different when you...' I nearly said 'grow up', but realised this would sound too hostile or defensive. 'When you meet the right har,' I said.

'Perhaps,' Gesaril said. At that point, he spotted

somehar more interesting than me and wandered off. I felt shaken, as if we'd just had a big fight.

Despite Gesaril, there were good times during those weeks I was with pearl. Orphie gradually responded to my coaxing, like a nervous stray fawn. He spent a lot of time with me, helping me at the vineyard, and at the house. I thought he must have had a very close relationship with his hostling and missed this har. Sometimes, he'd come over in the evening and snuggle up to me on the sofa, seeking comfort. I wasn't completely sure how I felt about that. It made me think about how soon I'd have a son of my own who'd want to do that kind of thing. I just couldn't see myself in that situation. But I can't deny there was something rewarding about the trust Orphie placed in me.

Ysobi was pleased about our friendship. 'Orphie needs to be drawn out,' he said. 'He and his hostling had a rough time for a while. It affected him.'

'What happened?'

Ysobi shrugged. 'I don't know exactly, but the hostling's dead now. Orphie doesn't like to talk about it, and I won't push it. He'll talk when he's ready.'

A wave of cold washed through me. 'That explains a lot.'

'You're doing him good. Thank you.'

'Yet more training for me,' I said. 'It's useful, I suppose.'

Ysobi pulled me close. 'I like it when we can work together like this.' He paused. 'But don't look on Orphie as a harling, Jass. He isn't. He hides behind appearing that way and that's not what he needs now.

I think, maybe, if you want to, you could help me with the arunic part of his training. He trusts you.'

'Is that soon?'

Ysobi nodded. 'It's overdue, actually. I thought he needed more time.'

I considered this for a moment and then came to a decision. 'Let me start it for him,' I said. 'You said yourself I could be a hienama one day.'

Ysobi kissed my forehead. 'You could. How about us starting tomorrow?'

'Well, better sooner rather than later.' I sighed. 'I'm not sure how much longer I'll be any good for such work.'

'It won't hurt our pearl, I know that.'

I went to the Nayati the following afternoon. Orphie was sitting in Ysobi's living room, looking as if he were about to be tortured to death. 'I'm not good at this stuff,' he told me, hands plunged deep between his knees.

'It's not about being good or bad,' I said. 'You don't have to do anything taxing today. I'm not going to hurt you. I'll just show you some things. OK?'

He nodded gravely. I saw then what Ysobi meant. Orphie did play act at being younger than he was. He would need careful handling.

Ysobi came in then, and we spent some minutes teaching Orphie about breath control and how to sense a har's energy field. Although Ysobi didn't include the sharing of breath in his training, I felt it was appropriate for Orphie, since it could act as a kind of gentle anaesthetic, and helped to lower inhibitions. Ysobi sat quietly while I initiated this. Orphie was the first har I'd touched since Ysobi and I had bonded. It felt strange, but not disloyal. I appreciated then, a little of what Ysobi had tried to make me understand about the student/hienama relationship.

Ysobi kept silent and let me do what I felt was right. He didn't interfere throughout any of it. Orphie seemed relaxed enough with the breath-sharing, so I continued it for quite some time. Then, when I judged the moment was right, I laid him back and began gently to undress him. Orphie whimpered a little and became tense. I stroked him, and murmured words to soothe him. 'We don't have to do this now,' I said. 'If you want to stop, we stop.'

He stared at me. 'No. I want to do this. I'm just nervous.'

'There's nothing to be nervous of. You're not a harling any more. You're made for this.'

He held my gaze. 'The feelings that aruna brings... they're too powerful. It's like you could get lost in them.'

I sat back on my heels, concerned. 'Did something bad happen to you, Orphie?' I asked softly.

He shook his head. 'Not to me, no. I want to get over this. Can we just go slowly?'

I nodded. 'Of course.' After a pause, I said, 'Is there anything you want to talk about first?'

'No,' Orphie replied. 'Let's just get on with it. What must I do?'

'Just relax. Let me do everything.'

He smiled at me, uncertainly. 'OK.'

It felt very odd having Ysobi watch me do things to Orphie that once he'd done to me. I was conscious of his eyes upon me. Orphie was not like Zehn; he

was difficult to arouse. Without asking Ysobi's advice, I
settled for working on one sikra, very softly. The sikra
was small and weak, difficult to find. After I felt it swell
just a little, I said to Orphie, 'Do you feel that?'

He nodded, eyes shut tight.

'I want you to imagine your whole being going
into that spot. Just relax. We'll take aruna now, but
pay attention to what happens inside you. OK?'

'Yes.'

I knelt up and pulled him onto my lap, held him
close. I went inside him carefully. He put his head on
my shoulder. Gradually, his initial shuddering sighs
became deeper. He began to move upon me. I fell
backwards, let him take control. By this time, he was
confident enough to do so. I knew I should be saying
things about control of energy and so on, but was just
pleased to see him taking aruna with abandon.
Training could come later, I thought. This was what he
needed now. I felt the tide building up within me and
closed my eyes. It was then I realised that my son was
aware of it too. It was like honey to him. My ouana-
tongue lashed out and Orphie contracted very strongly
about me. He bore down on me with all his weight,
pulling me deeper. He uttered deep grunts of
repletion. When he'd finished, he brushed damp hair
back from his face and smiled at me. I could tell he
didn't want to get off me. 'Keep going,' I whispered.
'It's OK.'

He closed his eyes and threw back his head. After
a while, he peaked again, and laughed aloud, pleased
with himself.

Orphie climbed off me and lay at my side. I pulled
him against me. 'I saw your pearl,' he said. 'It's a

golden sun inside you.' I think we had both forgotten Ysobi was there.

He came to us now and lay on my other side. 'I want you,' he said and pressed his mouth against my own.

It probably did Orphie good, seeing us taking aruna together like that. For a short time, Gesaril did not exist, and I gave myself to the har I loved, completely. Orphie lay beside me, stroking my hair. I turned my head to him once and he kissed me. 'You are so beautiful,' he said.

I know Ysobi would never have done anything like that, if it hadn't been for me. He let Orphie see the emotional side of aruna as well as the practical, magical side. He kept telling me he loved me and his release, when it came, was loud. Naked Ysobi. Few of his students had seen, or ever would see, that.

I felt a lot more secure after that day, even to the point of asking how things with Gesaril were going. Ysobi and I were out in my garden, in the evening time. Crows yelled at each other in the tall beeches of the sheep field. It was chill after dark, but I'd put a couple of lanterns on the old wooden table, so we could sit out there. I liked to smell the scents of the season; the potential of spring.

'He's a problem through and through,' Ysobi said. 'I've managed to reach him, to the point where he actually wants to work on himself, but that's brought other dilemmas. He feels vulnerable now, full of thoughts and feelings he doesn't understand.'

'Did he have a bad childhood or something?' What I really wanted to say was: I hope he's hurting to hell.

Ysobi shrugged. 'Not as far as I can tell, but he's an impenetrable har. His thoughts are always shielded. I think he just turned out the way he is. He's like an incepted har, in many ways. Even though Orphie needs cautious treatment, he's not unhinged. I think Gesaril might be.'

'What do you mean?' I was delighted to hear negative things about the har.

Ysobi gestured. 'Well, for one thing, he keeps feeling odd, disorientated. It's got to the point where I'm wary of leading him into any kind of meditation, since it affects him so dramatically. He came to me the other day and said that he'd been walking in the fields, and then a feeling stole over him. He couldn't remember where he was, or how he'd got there. He panicked, and found his way back to town.'

I tried not to sound too sceptical. 'Then he remembered where he was?'

Ysobi nodded. 'Yes. He said it was like waking up. He has a lot of bad dreams, too. Often, he's not sure what's real and what isn't. He's obviously sensitive to energies beyond normal perception, and part of him wants to shut that off. I wonder what he's hiding, or even if there is anything to hide. He's a puzzle.'

'So do you think you'll be able to sort him out?' I asked.

'I hope so. It seems the more he learns, the more the world feels like an alien place to him. I've even considered writing to the Academy at Kyme. A second opinion might be useful.'

I knew Ysobi believed he was good at his job, and it would take a lot for him to want another har's verdict on one of his students. Perhaps Gesaril really was screwed up, and his behaviour wasn't just an act to gain attention.

'I decided to stall the arunic training,' Ysobi said. 'I think that was contributing to his state of mind.'

Thank the dehara for that. 'Oh,' I said nonchalantly. 'Will there come a point where you just give up and send him home?'

Ysobi laughed. 'Come on, Jass. Do you really think I'd do that?'

Orphie happened to be there when the pearl arrived. He came to my door one afternoon just before the equinox, knowing I'd be at home. Some days before, Sinnar had told me not to come to work again until after it was all over and the harling had emerged from the pearl. He'd listen to no argument otherwise. I knew the time was soon, because my insides felt so peculiar, so I was just taking things easy. I was surprised to see Orphie though, since this was his training time. I reflected how much older and more confident he looked now and felt warm inside because I knew I'd helped him. We had a special connection, but it wasn't an unhealthy thing. Orphie was not the obsessive type.

'Ysobi sent me away,' Orphie said as soon as I'd shut the kitchen door behind him.

'Oh? Why's that?' I asked him, indicating he should sit at the table.

'Gesaril came,' Orphie muttered darkly. He looked genuinely displeased and wouldn't sit down.

'What do you mean?'

Orphie gestured angrily with both hands. 'We

were in the middle of things, and then Gesaril just burst into the room. He didn't apologise, or even seem to notice I was there. He was hysterical. I was naked. It was really embarrassing. Ysobi tried to calm Gesaril down, but he was out of his mind. Then Ysobi told *me* to leave.'

I swallowed, aware that my heart-rate had increased, although I strove to keep my voice light. 'Well, that's understandable, Orphie. Don't take it personally. I think Gesaril's a bit sick in the head.'

'I think he's jealous!' Orphie blurted. His face had gone red.

I went cold. 'Jealous? Why?'

'He did it on purpose because he knew what we were doing. I'm sure of it. He doesn't like Ysobi training me. It's not right. My phyle is paying Jesith just as much as Gesaril's parents are for training. I feel like I'm second best, always!'

I hesitated. 'Orphie, has Gesaril interrupted your training sessions more than once?'

Orphie nodded. 'He often turns up. Not when we're doing arunic arts, though, except for today. It was like he just couldn't stop himself. Usually, he'll just come into the room when we're meditating or performing majhahn, and lurk about. I don't like it. He's a distraction. He makes me feel nervous and I can't concentrate. Ysobi never tells him to go, and I wish he would.'

I heard in those last words an unspoken plea for me to speak on his behalf. I was angry with Ysobi, because he couldn't see that Orphie was suffering while he tried so desperately to sort out Gesaril. I couldn't speak frankly to one of his students, much as

I'd have liked to grill Orphie for more details, so just said airily: 'Don't worry, Orphie. Yz probably doesn't realise you can't work with Gesaril there. I'll speak to him for you, then it'll stop. OK?'

Orphie hugged me. 'Thank you, Jass. I knew you would.' He regarded me steadily. 'Gesaril has a thing for Ysobi, but I suppose you know that.'

I laughed, and hoped it didn't sound off key. 'I know that, Orphie. It's just a crush.'

'I think it's more creepy than that.'

I stared at Orphie, torn between speaking openly to him and maintaining a professional distance. We were friends, but because he was one of Ysobi's students, I thought it wasn't right for me to confide in him about my personal life. In hindsight, I was stupid. I'd once shared an intensely intimate moment with Orphie, and was shortly about to do so again, albeit in a different sense. 'Well,' I said lightly, 'if anything ever creeps you *particularly*, you can come and tell me about it.'

'I'm not just being spiteful,' Orphie said. 'Don't think that.'

'I don't.' I smiled in heatless cheer, and was about to offer Orphie a drink to change the subject, when suddenly a hurricane of pain blew over me, or rather hit me like a fist. I staggered backwards against the table, clutching my stomach.

'What is it?' Orphie asked.

I swallowed, took a deep breath, and when I spoke, it was with difficulty. 'Take my pony. Ride to the vineyard. Fetch Sinnar.'

Orphie's eyes had gone completely round. 'Is it the pearl?'

'Hurry!' I said.

Orphie ran out of the door, leaving it open behind him. Moments later, I saw him gallop past, riding my pony bareback, with only a rope halter to steer him with. Fortunately, the beast's most familiar journey was to the vineyard and back, so a lack of a bridle wouldn't be a problem for a rider who didn't know him. I leaned back against the table. I dared not move. I was sure I could hear my body creaking and groaning.

I'd already been informed that a pearl drop can take quite a long time; we're not so different from humans in that respect. Sinnar came almost at once – he must have ridden like a maniac – and got me upstairs. Orphie had come back with him, and now Sinnar shouted orders at him, telling him what items he'd need, and so on.

'Fetch Yz,' I said to Orphie. 'Fetch him now.'

Orphie hesitated. I could see he didn't want to do it. Then he nodded. 'OK. I'll be right back.'

Sinnar arranged me on the bed. He put towels beneath my hips and I found myself thinking of that first time with Ysobi. For some reason, this upset me. 'I don't want this,' I said. 'Sinnar, I don't want any of this.'

'Hush.' He stroked my forehead. 'I'm going to make you an herbal drink, and it'll make you feel better. Just keep breathing deeply.'

I took hold of his wrist. 'You're our phylarch. You shouldn't be doing this. It seems... I don't know... wrong.'

'I look on it as part of my job,' he said. 'What

should the harish term be for mid-wife, do you think? Mid-har doesn't sound right. But anyway, I like doing this, so let me go.'

Left alone, I felt as if I was in shock again. It was real now. In hours, perhaps sooner, a pearl would come out of me. There was life inside me. It seemed so unlikely. Did I really want a harling? Would I have to take it to work with me? I'd pushed to the back of my mind any thoughts concerning how it would affect my life. At Natalia, I'd just been ensorcelled by the romantic idea, and now I was alone, and in pain, and Ysobi was somewhere else, comforting Gesaril.

I was weeping by the time Sinnar came back upstairs. 'I'm so stupid,' I said to him. 'I'm so fucking stupid.'

'Drink this,' he said, holding out a steaming mug. 'You're not stupid.'

I took a sip of the hot murky liquid, then spat it out. 'That's vile! I don't want it!'

'Yes you do. Don't think about it. Just swallow it. You'll be grateful afterwards.'

He was right. Whatever Sinnar had put into that drink, it was a hefty dose. I could observe the pain, but it was as if it wasn't me feeling it; very strange.

Orphie came back alone. He slunk into the room and came to stand beside the bed. He didn't say anything at first.

'Where's Yz?' I asked him.

'He says he'll be here soon,' Orphie answered. He looked pained.

'When?'

Orphie shrugged. 'Can I help, tiahaar?' he asked Sinnar. 'I know about this. I helped with my brother's pearl.'

'I didn't know you had a brother,' Sinnar said. He said it in a way that implied he thought Orphie was all alone in the world.

'Why isn't Ysobi here?' I moaned. 'Sinnar, why isn't he here? Will you fetch him for me?'

'Sssh.' Sinnar gripped one of my hands. 'I can't leave now.'

'You can if you want,' Orphie said. 'I know what to do.' And he said that in a way that implied he really thought Sinnar should go to the Nayati.

'He'll come when he's ready,' Sinnar said. He and Orphie stared at one another, and it appeared that some unspoken dialogue occurred.

'He's with that shitsucker,' I announced. 'His welfare is more important than mine.'

Even in my deranged state, it didn't escape me that Sinnar knew precisely who I was talking about, since he didn't question me about it. 'Don't worry about anything but yourself and the pearl,' he said. 'Yz will be here, Jass. You know he will.'

Orphie looked as if he was bursting to say something, but held his tongue.

'Go and watch the water, Orphie,' Sinnar said. 'I put a large pan on the stove. It needs to be boiled.'

Orphie left the room.

'Sinnar,' I said. 'Speak to me honestly. Do I have a problem?'

'It's all fine,' Sinnar said. 'I'll massage some ointment into your soume-lam. It'll make things easier.'

'That's not what I meant.'

'Now's not the time, Jass.'

'Yes it is. Answer me. Is there something I don't know?'

Sinnar shook his head vigorously. 'No, no. You don't have the problem. Ysobi does. Tibar really regrets asking him to train Gesaril now. Everyhar can see he's screwed up. Ysobi can't bear to fail, that's the trouble. We all think he's investing too much time and energy into a hopeless case, and that's all it is. Gesaril's no threat to you, Jass. Now, try to relax. Let's concentrate on the task in hand.'

I was lucky: the entire procedure took less than two hours. I was out of my mind on Sinnar's herbal concoction, and the first time I saw the pearl I laughed. 'It looks like a big nut or a fruit,' I said. 'It's bizarre.' I wondered what the harling would look like now, if I cut open the pearl with a knife. One minute I was laughing hysterically, the next I was weeping. I was sitting on blood-soaked towels that were going cold. Sinnar gave me another drink. I was semi-conscious as he and Orphie dealt with the bed and then put me into it.

I must have slept. When I woke up, Orphie was sitting in a chair beside the bed, reading a book by the dim light of my lamp. It seemed as if many hours had passed. The room still smelled of blood. 'Where's Ysobi?' I asked.

Orphie looked at me and put down his book. He came to sit on the bed and took one of my hands. 'He came, but you were asleep.'

'You mean he came and went?'

Orphie nodded. I turned my head away. Sinnar was a liar.

'He looked at the pearl,' Orphie said. 'Do you want to see it?'

'No. I know what it looks like.'

Orphie sighed. 'Quite a few of your friends have called, but Sinnar told me to send them all away until tomorrow. He's gone home for dinner now, but says he'll look in on you later. I'll stay the night with you, Jass.'

I squeezed his fingers, but could not speak.

'You should have the pearl in bed with you, really,' Orphie said. 'It's wrapped up, but I think body warmth helps it grow. I slept with my brother every night until he hatched.'

I looked at him then. 'What about your hostling? Why didn't he do it?'

Orphie looked away. 'He... he died. Something went wrong.'

'I'm sorry.'

'Yeah. I didn't want to tell you before, in case it frightened you, but it was different for him anyway.' He paused. 'You and Ysobi both know there's a reason I had problems with the arunic part of my training. I want to tell you about it now. Can I?'

I nodded.

'Thanks.' Orphie gazed at the wall, as if into the past. 'My hostling's name was Loruen. He was the travelling type, and we'd go from settlement to settlement, where he'd work for a while, then move on. I never got to meet my father, although Loruen said that one day he'd take me to him. Well, one time, we got into trouble, near Lund.'

Lund was renowned as a dangerous area in Alba Sulh. The worst elements gathered there, skulking in the ruins. I nodded again in encouragement.

Orphie swallowed. I could tell this was difficult for him. 'Some hara... wild hara... captured us. That happens, you know. To some, other hara are like... I don't know, just animals. I won't call *them* animals, because animals would never do the things they did. They wanted Loruen to take aruna with them, but they were so cruel. They jeered at him. He refused, which I think now was stupid, but that's just the way he was. He didn't like anyhar telling him what to do. So they just forced him anyway, and committed pelki on him. I had to watch. They beat him really badly.'

I didn't want to think that things like that happened here in Alba Sulh, the green land of magic. I didn't know what to say. But now that Orphie had broached the subject with somehar, he wanted to say it all.

'They made him with pearl somehow,' he said. 'I don't know how they did it, because he fought them all the way. I can't remember some of it now, because it went on for so long. I don't know how they did it.' He frowned.

'Maybe they gave him a drink, like the one Sinnar gave me earlier,' I said, dully.

Orphie nodded. 'Perhaps. Anyway, he was badly damaged. They put us in a hole in the ground and we were there for what seemed like days. Sometimes, they'd throw food down to us.'

'How did you get away?' I asked.

Orphie sighed. 'We were very lucky. Some other hara came along and raided the nest we'd been taken to, so we were rescued. They were from a local settlement, and they'd heard rumours there were captives nearby, so they'd come to find out if it was true. We were cared for, and they did everything they could, but Loruen died when the pearl came out of him. He bled to death. It was like more of him came out than should have done. The healers could do nothing. I was there. Now you know.'

I was glad he hadn't revealed those facts to me before. But how to react? It wasn't easy. 'I'm so sorry, Orphie. I don't know what to say.'

'Congratulate me,' he said bitterly. 'I was next on the list, but I escaped. I was told that our captors were probably waiting for my feybraiha. They liked to seize hara to use them for breeding, so they didn't have the inconvenience of having pearls themselves.' Orphie grimaced. 'Some hara are hideous. When I'm around Gesaril, I get the same feelings I used to get in that nest. It's like a smell of burning hair.'

I shuddered. 'What happened when you went back to the Nayati earlier?' I asked. 'Tell me the truth.'

Orphie looked me in the eye. 'Gesaril had done something bad to himself.'

'What do you mean?'

'I don't know the details, but there was blood. I think he cut himself. Ysobi had Tibar there, and a couple of the other hienamas. I didn't see much, because they'd got Gesaril in the bedroom, but Tibar said Gesaril was hurt.'

'How clever of him,' I said.

'Yeah,' Orphie agreed. He reached out and stroked my face. 'Do you want anything, like a drink, or something to eat?'

'In a while,' I said. 'Thanks, Orphie.'

'You're welcome.' He smiled. 'Thanks for

listening. I don't speak about my past to many hara. I don't like them knowing. There's no need for them to know.'

'I understand,' I said. 'It won't go any further.'

'You can tell Ysobi,' Orphie said. 'I suppose I should tell him myself but...' He looked at me meaningfully. 'It's easier with you.'

I reached out and squeezed one of his hands. 'I'll respect that.'

Orphie smiled. 'You know, I've made a decision. When I go out into the world, I'm going to find a har like you to be chesna with, and I'll bring him back here to meet you.'

'I'd like that. I know you'll find yourself a wondrous har, Orphie.'

'I'll never forget your goodness,' he said. 'Shall I fetch the pearl now?'

'I suppose so.'

'It's not the harling's fault,' Orphie said.

Ysobi did not come to see me until the morning, but at least he arrived early. I'd waited for him all night, getting more and more anxious by the minute. I'd asked Orphie to go back to the Nayati, but he wouldn't. No matter how much I pleaded, he remained obstinate. When Ysobi finally did turn up, he looked wretched, with dark marks beneath his eyes. His hair was lank. I wanted both to hug and hit him. I was so angry that I couldn't speak, since anything I did say would come out as an incoherent rant.

Ysobi sat by the bed. He looked so serious. A tremor of fear went through me. I thought he was going to tell me our chesna bond was over. There was a distance between us. 'I'm sorry, Jass,' he said.

Still, I could not speak.

'You probably know what happened.'

I shook my head, and then found my voice. 'I only know what happened to me. I don't care about anything else.'

'I should have been with you, I know,' he said. 'But I couldn't, Jass. I couldn't leave a student of mine in such a terrible state, and I knew you had Sinnar and Orphie with you, perhaps others. You have lots of friends, who care for you deeply. Gesaril has nohar.'

'He has you,' I pointed out sourly.

Ysobi didn't dispute that, which only made me angrier.

'And you might as well drop the "my student" thing, Yz,' I said coldly. 'He's Gesaril to you, a har, not just a student.' I sighed, and it hurt my chest. 'I suppose we have to talk. I need to know what's changed. We have to talk about the future, because of what we've created.'

'Nothing's changed, and we'll talk about our son's future all you want.'

'If nothing's changed, then I want you to send Gesaril away.'

There was a deep uncomfortable silence.

'I mean it, Yz. I'm tolerant. It's not just about being petty and jealous over you spending time with students. I don't mind about Orphie. But I do mind about the other one. He wants you. He's obsessed with you. And if you can't admit that, you're either blindly stupid or lying to yourself.'

Ysobi rubbed his face with both hands. 'You know I can't send him away, Jass. We've talked about all this. If you're truly my chesnari, you'll ride this out with me until Gesaril is ready to go home. You'll trust me.'

'He's dangerous. Can't you see that?'

Ysobi stared at me steadily. 'No, actually, I can't. He's damaged, but not dangerous. Why would you think such a thing? He's pathetic and to be pitied, if anything.'

These words did nothing but kindle my fury. 'Oh, really! Then answer this: Would the wise hienama Ysobi usually throw one of his students out, simply to cater to the demanding whims of another?'

Ysobi looked taken aback. 'What?'

'Orphie came to me yesterday. He was upset you'd thrown him out just because Gesaril barged in. You humiliated him, and that isn't like you. You should have ordered Gesaril out, not Orphie. And it's not just that. Orphie is confiding in me, when he should be confiding in you. You're ruining your professional relationship with him, and... excuse *me*... wasn't that once so *important* to you? What's wrong with you? Stand back and look at the situation, will you? It's unhealthy.'

Ysobi's expression had become hard. He didn't like to be criticised like this. 'I'm sorry Orphie was upset, and I'll speak to him about it, but Gesaril needed attention. I have to be there for him. I opened him up, and it's my responsibility to help him become whole. He needs me more than Orphie does.'

I actually snarled. 'He *needs* you? Listen to yourself! Yz, I think you need to examine this whole situation properly in your head, because to tell you the truth I'm really starting to suspect that you feel something other than teacherly concern for that har. If you want him, and it's the kind of want that excludes a chesna bond with me, then I have to know. I won't share you with him, Yz. You have to make a choice. He's saying the same thing to you, but in a different way. He's using emotional blackmail. He wants you to make a choice too.'

'You've done this,' Ysobi said, abruptly. It didn't sound like his voice. 'You made me open up too, and this is the result. I'd closed myself down to all involvement. Perhaps, when I let you seduce me, I forgot why I'd done that. Now, I remember.'

'Get out,' I said.

He didn't move.

'I mean it. *Get out!* The final two words were a shriek that was no doubt audible for a radius of several miles around the house.

Ysobi stared at me hard for some moments, then got up and left the room without another word. I heard him punch the wall in the hallway.

I was overwhelmed by grief, and wept uncontrollably for hours. Orphie came running to my side the minute Ysobi had left the house, but could do nothing to console me. By now, my friends must have realised something was wrong, because Orphie still wouldn't let them in the house – and it's not unlikely some of them heard me yelling. I didn't want to have to face Minnow or any others, because I was ashamed of my own stupidity, the insane notion I could have a life with Ysobi, the hienama of arunic arts. I wanted to pretend everything was all right. I didn't want pity. I had to make plans for the future. Would that involve leaving Jesith? I could leave the pearl with Ysobi. He'd made me have it; now he'd done this to me. Let's see how he'd cope with satisfying all the *needs* of his students with a harling to look after.

My dream of a life had just shattered.

However, in the early evening, Ysobi came back to me. He came into the room and stood staring at me for some moments. I must have looked a real mess, my eyes swollen from weeping. He, on the other hand, looked radiant. There was a fire in him.

'What I said to you earlier was unforgivable,' he said, 'as was the fact I wasn't here for you yesterday. I know you needed me too, and I was wrong to abandon you. I should have got Tibar to deal with Gesaril and have come to you instead. I won't ask you to accept an apology, but I am deeply sorry.'

He was going to say more, but shook his head, looked at the floor. It was at that moment I resolved I'd fight for him, and if I had to use wiles as underhand as Gesaril's then so be it. I stared at him with wide eyes that I willed to fill up with tears. I pulled back the blankets of the bed to show him the pearl lying beside me, as if it had been there all the time, which it hadn't. Orphie had had to bully me to warm it. Ysobi came to my bedside and knelt on the floor. He put his face in his hands.

'This is what's most important,' I murmured. 'It was made in love. We will be strong.'

He uttered a soft cry and fell upon me.

I held him close. 'Tell me what happened,' I said.

What happened was this. Ysobi had stayed overnight with me the night before the pearl arrived and while I'd slept he'd laid his hand on my stomach to feel the pearl. He liked to do that; more so than I did, anyway. He'd felt movement inside me, and psychically he'd begun to suspect my time was near. This feeling had nagged at him during the morning, and he'd decided he would come to me in the early afternoon. Then the episode with Gesaril had occurred. 'I intended to give him half an hour of my time,' Ysobi said. 'I intuited Orphie would come to you, so I knew you wouldn't be alone, but it wasn't my intention not to be part of the pearl drop.'

'So he hurt himself to keep you there?' I asked.

Ysobi sighed. 'I tried to dismiss him, as gently as I could. But he begged me not to leave the Nayati. He said he was terrified of something and he wasn't making it up, Jass. I could tell. He said he could see faces all around him that wished to harm him.'

Ysobi had been firm, or so he told me. He'd told Gesaril that there were no evil influences around him. But Gesaril wouldn't accept this. He'd reminded Ysobi that he was responsible for his students. In return, Ysobi had told Gesaril that most of his fears were in his imagination, and he'd got to start taking more responsibility for himself. He'd also said why he wanted to come to me, which perhaps had been a mistake. Eventually, Gesaril had calmed down and left the room. He'd spoken about wanting to use the bathroom before he left.

What he'd actually done was go straight to the kitchen and hack at his wrists and throat with the sharpest blade he could find. I imagine it made quite a mess.

I didn't want to hear what Gesaril had said, as Ysobi – and later Tibar and the other hienamas – had patched him up. But Ysobi wanted to tell me so I had to listen. 'If I'm dead, I won't be a bother to you any more. I won't be a bother to anyhar. Let me die.' And so on.

Was this really a plea from the heart from a damaged soul or a calculated dramatic act? I wondered if I was just exceptionately hard-hearted and cold. After all, here I was, surrounded by supporters and Gesaril was lying alone, virtually under guard, in a bedroom of the Nayati. Ysobi was here with me and I held against my side the one thing that was perhaps my most potent weapon in this war. If it was a war.

3

At least Ysobi accepted that Gesaril was too reliant on him, and agreed to let Sinnar monitor the har for the next few days. Gesaril was removed to the phylarch's house, and Ysobi carried on working with Orphie. I knew Orphie was disgusted by the whole affair and shared my views. But that might just have been because he cared for me.

I was unaware of public opinion over the Gesaril business, or even how much others in the community knew about it, but my friends tactfully kept quiet on the subject. They came to visit me all the time, and one night, I got blissfully drunk with Fahn, Minnow and Vole. We laughed a lot. There was no mention of Gesaril.

Ysobi came to stay with me more often. Once, I said to him, 'Will Gesaril be sent home now?'

Ysobi hesitated before answering. 'We've sent a letter to Kyme.'

'Meaning?' A hard edge had come into my voice. I couldn't help it.

'We can't just abandon him, Jass.'

I thought I could abandon him quite easily, preferably naked, on an exposed hillside during a snowstorm. 'Are you still going to try and work with him?'

'He has to work on himself, mainly. I think most of his fears are imaginary.'

'You think it's possible to help him, then?'

'I don't think it's impossible.'

I wanted to say more, but held my tongue. I'd decided that arguments should not be part of my arsenal.

Before I continue with the story of Gesaril, there has to be an interlude. I have to talk about my son.

The harling came into our lives properly about a week after the equinox. I noticed the pearl had gone brittle and cracks appeared in it. Transfixed, I put it on the kitchen table and sat next to it, watching. I drank some wine as I did so. Eventually, it fell apart completely and a weird little animal crawled out. We stared at each other for some moments. It was most disorientating. I said, 'Hello, creature,' and the harling lifted its head, on a neck that seemed a little too long and thin, and sniffed the air. I had some cream cheese in the cold room and went to fetch it.

When I returned, after only a few seconds, the harling was examining the broken pieces of the pearl. He turned quickly, defensively, when he heard me approach. I offered the cheese and he ate it from my hand like a wary horse, flinching back if I made any sudden movements. I could not imagine how this creature could in any way grow to be a har. He was intelligent, that was obvious, and more like a colt or a calf than a cub or a pup, since he could move about and eat immediately after hatching. He was alien to behold because he wasn't at all like a human baby, but more like an older child in miniature form. He had a sense of survival and cunning. His first noises were hisses.

Orphie found me attempting communication with my alien son. He walked in through the kitchen door, stiffened in horror at what he beheld, and said, 'Jass, it's freezing in here! The window's open. Get a blanket for the harling. He needs bathing as well. Are you mad?'

'I don't know what to do,' I said. 'Look at him.'

Orphie picked the harling up. At first he struggled and hissed, then became quiet. 'He's shivering,' Orphie said. 'Get a blanket, Jass.'

'He's had some cheese,' I said. Then I went to fetch a blanket.

In the bedroom, I nearly passed out. I'd given birth and it was a monster. Somehow I got back downstairs.

The harling was asleep in Orphie's arms and now appeared less alien. He was covered in a viscous fluid, which must have protected him inside the pearl. I saw then he had an umbilical cord, or rather had once had, as it appeared Orphie had cut it. Orphie wrapped the blanket I'd brought around the harling; it draped down to the floor. 'Are you drunk?' Orphie asked, rather sharply.

I shook my head. 'No. I'm just concussed by life.'

'It's a good job I'm here, then. Get some warm water. We'll bathe him.'

We dabbed at the sleeping harling with wet cloths and as I did so, I was thinking: *This came out of me. This is mine.* I thought I should be feeling something more than shock.

Strangely enough, I didn't consider sending Orphie to fetch Ysobi. I was content for it just to be

Orphie and me dealing with this unhinging event.

'He'll sleep a lot at first,' Orphie said. 'And eat, of course. They grow very quick, Jass. You can almost see it happening.'

'We don't know each other,' I said. 'How does it work, all that hostling stuff? Shouldn't I be feeling sentimental or something?'

'I'll help you,' Orphie said. And that was that.

I named him Zephyrus, for the wind that had blown in through the open kitchen window, right over him as he'd crawled from the pearl. It shortened nicely to Zeph. When Ysobi was staying overnight, he slept in his own room, but when I was alone he'd slither under my blankets and curl up on my chest like a cat, an ear pressed to the place where my heart was beating beneath the skin. It was a strange relationship we had, a sort of mutual wary respect that I hoped would one day turn into affection and trust. He trusted me completely, but I didn't trust him. I thought he might try to smother me in my sleep. It was because he had a thinking mind and I didn't know what was in it. Surely, a hostling should be closer psychically to his son than I was? Zeph was part of me and yet not. I couldn't hear his thoughts, even when I tried really hard. One night, I woke from a dream of falling. I woke up gasping, my limbs twitching. Of course, Zeph was on my chest, like an incubus of nightmare; too heavy. He woke up too and murmured, 'Sleep, Jassy. Good.' Then he settled down again.

They were his first words. I'd have been less surprised if my pony had said my name, I think.

Zeph followed me around, or Ysobi, or Orphie, as

if he was a duckling following the mother duck. He
tended to regard all three of us as equally responsible
for him. On the nights Ysobi was with us, Zeph would
sleep in his own room without getting out of bed and
wandering around. He was too sensible to do things
that were dangerous to his body, like human children
often did. He'd come to the vineyard with me and
suck at the preserved fruits on the table where I
worked, his fingers and lips stained blackberry purple.
He'd sit in the Nayati while Orphie and Ysobi were
meditating, and there he liked to play with water; the
fountains in the garden, the shallow pool filled with
water lilies and sleek black fish. We quickly learned he
had a thing about water. He was not particularly fond
of strangers and seemed to prefer a small group of
friends, or rather family. He was impatient when hara
tried to fuss over or handle him and would usually spit
at them if they tried it, or else run up the curtains like
a cat, which often almost terrified hara. Despite this,
other hara liked him. You couldn't really help it: in his
face was the beauty he would one day become. He
would permit only Orphie and me to hug him,
although he did like to climb Ysobi's legs and cling to a
thigh as his father walked around. Occasionally, he'd
climb further, like a kitten, until he was perched on
Ysobi's shoulders. He liked Ysobi's hair and enjoyed
biting and chewing it.

This creature, this little alien, was a marvel. I
enjoyed discovering his developing quirks and
preferences. Sometimes, we'd both stop what we were
doing and stare at each other for some moments: I
think we both wondered what we felt, and what we
should feel. One day I said to him, 'I think I love you,

after all.'

He nodded. 'Yes.' He reached out to pat my face, as if to tell me everything was all right.

But it was not all right. Not yet. Zeph knew nothing about more adult concerns, of course. But others did.

It might have been coincidence, but the bad dreams I'd had when Ysobi had first initiated arunic arts with Gesaril returned. They were hideous waking dreams, when I'd wake up into utter blackness and sense there was something malevolent in the room with me. Sometimes, I'd hear voices outside the house, even though beyond my window there was no longer any world, only a spinning void. I'd catch my breath, then wake up and find I'd been dreaming. I'd get out of bed and go down to the kitchen to get a drink, but when I reached the bottom of the stairs, blackness would creep in on me again and I wouldn't be alone. I'd catch my breath and wake up again. The sequence could happen many times in a row and lasted for what seemed like hours of torment.

I told Sinnar about it, wondering if it was an after-effect of pearl bearing, and he seemed to think it might be. 'You've had to adjust dramatically to the soume aspect of your being,' he said. 'Even though you've assimilated it on the surface, I think you're still churning things around, deep inside.'

To help me, one afternoon we performed a simple majhahn of healing together in a private open-air Nayati, deep in a part of the woods not many hara used. Neither he nor I mentioned our intentions to anyhar, which at the time I didn't really question, although now it seems strange. We called upon the dehara, and visited the astral realm in meditation. Sinnar guided our inner journey to the astral palace of Aruhani, who although is a dehar of aruna, birth and death, also has a vicious side. Sinnar asked him to protect me.

When we came out of the meditation, I asked him why he'd done that. 'Do I need protection?' I asked.

'Sometimes we need protection from ourselves,' he answered. It was a bright winter day, but freezing cold. We sat upon large stones that had been arranged in a circle to create the boundary of the Nayati.

I shivered, and pulled my goatskin coat closer around me. The long goat hair around my neck moved in the wind. I was surrounded by a smell of animal that was turning to carrion. 'The dreams I have...' I almost didn't want to speak, and I noticed Sinnar wasn't too keen to meet my eye. 'They could be a symptom of psychic attack, right?'

'I'm sure it's not that,' Sinnar said. He looked at me then. 'You're strong. It would take a very strong soul to reach you in that way.'

I put my head to one side, raised an eyebrow. '*Sinnar*,' I said meaningfully.

He sighed. 'I meant what I said. I don't know anyhar capable of hurting you... who would want to.'

Yet still he'd felt the need to add that little coda to our ritual. I didn't want to believe it was possible either. I didn't want Gesaril to have the ability to wield that kind of power.

I said nothing of that afternoon to Ysobi, or to anyhar else, but I kept alert. I watched for signs and omens, I prowled my house like a cat after dark, but unfortunately I paid less attention to what was going on in my inner world.

A new student had arrived; a boisterous young har called Aeron, who had recently been incepted into a phyle further east. He was not dislikeable, although a handful in a different way to how Gesaril was. He was of the type that thought he knew everything, and tended to challenge Ysobi and argue with him. I think Ysobi rather enjoyed this. In appearance, Aeron was long-faced and thin, a har not yet altogether comfortable in his new skin. I could tell he was unable to see beauty in himself, which was probably why he was so stroppy. If you complimented him, he'd get aggressive in his embarrassment. For this reason, hara used to tease him a lot. Most of the time, he didn't know whether to shout at them or cry. I thought it prudent to invite Aeron to dinner sometimes too, as we did with Orphie. Ysobi was spending a lot more time with the students; Orphie and Aeron worked well together, surprisingly. Consequently, I was beginning to go out in the evenings alone, or rather I took Zeph with me. If he got tired, he'd find a corner near my feet and go to sleep. If he was awake, he'd watch hara and occasionally condescend to interact with them, if he was in the mood. It was almost as if Gesaril had left Jesith: nohar talked about him, and I never saw him about. I assumed Sinnar had him under control, and once Kyme had sent word about him, a decision as to his future would be made. My bad dreams diminished after the majhahn I'd done with Sinnar; maybe our secret fears had been misplaced.

One evening, Zehn and I had an argument. To be more accurate, Zehn once again took it upon himself to take me on. No, that's not accurate at all. I'll just say what happened.

I'd gone to Willow Pool Garden to see one of the inevitable travelling bands that played there regularly. Most of my friends were there and I joined their group. Spring was surging over the land and everyhar was in high spirits. Zeph was feeling sociable too, which meant we both got a lot of attention. I noticed Zehn come in. He cast me a glance and stared at me expressionlessly for some moments – I was laughing loudly at some joke or another. Then he shook his head. He went to the bar. I stared after him for a few seconds, then forgot it. Zehn was Zehn. There was nothing I could do about it. After he'd downed a few drinks, he came to my table and sat down.

'Where's Arken?' I asked him.

'Where's Ysobi?' he asked back.

'Working,' I said. 'So?'

Again, Zehn shook his head. He fixed me with a stare, and a feeling like cold water ran down my spine.

'What is it?' I asked.

'I want to talk to you,' he said. 'Somehar has to.'

'Talk, then.'

'Not here. Outside. Leave the harling with Fahn.'

I resented these orders at once. 'Tell me here,' I said. By this time, a few ears were beginning to tune into our conversation. I sensed a stillness sweep over the group like a softly spreading plague.

'You don't want me to talk to you here, trust me,' Zehn said.

I bristled. 'Then maybe I don't want to hear what you've got to say.'

Fahn, who had Zeph on his lap, said, 'Is

everything OK, Jass?'

Zehn continued to stare at me. 'I need to talk to you,' he said, in a low voice. 'You must listen.' He softened. 'Please.'

I got to my feet. 'All right.' I turned to Fahn. 'Would you watch Zeph for a minute?'

Fahn was frowning, perplexed. 'Of course.'

My son held out a hand to me. He looked furious. 'Don't,' he said.

I touched the ends of his reaching fingers. 'I'll be five minutes at most, I promise.'

Zehn and I went out front, onto the street. Hara were still strolling through the evening, making for the bar. I heard the band start playing; a roll of drums. There was a spreading communal lawn in front of us, shivering with daffodils. The air tasted green in my mouth. A rangy greyhound was nosing through the flowers, wagging his tail.

Zehn and I sat on a stone bench beneath the eaves of the bar. Zehn was silent at first, so I had to say, 'What is it, then?'

He rubbed his hands through his hair. 'Somehar has to tell you,' he said.

I didn't say the obvious. I kept quiet, although that cold water down my back was turning slowly to ice.

'Ysobi is still seeing Gesaril,' he said.

I kept calm. 'Understandably. The har's in a state and Ysobi's his teacher.'

'No, Jass.' Zehn groaned. 'You're going to think this is just sour grapes, I know, but there are things you should know. Tibar told me. Everyhar knows.'

'OK,' I said slowly. 'Explain exactly what you mean.'

'On the nights Ysobi's not with you, he's with Gesaril. He does it secretly, only Tibar saw him sneaking out of the house one morning. He did a bit of detective work after that. Discovered it's a regular thing.'

It was the secretiveness that distressed me, although I didn't show it. I didn't know what to say, really. I had a flashback to dropping the pearl, a twinge of pain.

'I'm sorry, but I think you should know,' Zehn said.

'What makes you think I don't?' I said.

Zehn raised his eyebrows. 'You can't be serious.'

'A chesna bond is different,' I said. 'I'm not selfish with him, Zehn.'

'I don't believe you. You're lying. You didn't know.'

'Well, think what you like. I'm going back inside now.'

I stood up. I really meant to leave him sitting there, but he grabbed my arm. 'You're stupid,' he said. 'Do you think you're the first?'

'Let me go!'

'No!' Zehn grabbed my other arm. 'You have to listen, Jass. The last time... we all liked him, really liked him, in the same way we like you. We had to watch Ysobi destroy him. Nohar intervened. Now he's not here anymore.'

'What are you saying?' I asked coldly. 'Is he dead?'

Zehn shook his head. 'No. At least, not physically. He left Jesith.'

I sat down again. 'What was his name?'

'Mori... Morien.'

'When?'

'About two years ago.'

That recently? I swallowed with difficulty. 'I suppose you'd better tell me.'

'It was the same,' Zehn said. 'It always is. Mori wasn't the first either. I've not been here that long, but you get to hear things. It's a pattern, Jass.'

'Did this Mori have a harling with Yz?'

'No. That's irrelevant. Ysobi got together with Mori, and it was different in some ways. They didn't socialise, like you do; well, not together. But Mori was smitten with him. It was the same story; the aruna training. It blew Mori's mind away. He fell in love. And then another student came. I don't need to tell you more. You can guess it.'

'This is not the same, Zehn. It really isn't.'

'Oh, open your eyes!' Zehn yelled. 'Don't you get it? All that ascetic teacher stuff is bullshit! Ysobi gets off on hara adoring him. He makes it happen. I'm sure he wants the chesna bond, when it happens, but then another needy, pretty face shows up and he can't resist doing what he does. It's a power trip. You have to face it and accept it.'

'No, I don't,' I said. 'You've told me. I'll discuss it with him. Now I'm really going back inside.'

'Don't be a fool,' Zehn said. 'You have that harling now. Get out of the chesna state while you can. Finish it. You have friends, good friends. None of us want to see you go the same way Mori did.'

'You're in no position to lecture me about Ysobi's behaviour,' I said. 'Everyhar knows what you are. Maybe it takes one to know one? Or rather you're projecting your way of being onto Ysobi?'

Zehn did not get angrier, as I expected. He sighed. 'Jass, I'm no angel, I know that. I think you also know why... maybe. But I don't do this whole guru power thing. Never. I take aruna with hara, maybe too carelessly. I make them like me too much, I know. Perhaps I don't want commitment, or perhaps my standards are too high... I don't know. But I am *not* like him. When things go bad with my roon friends, they stick around, like Fahn. They don't run because they can't bear to stay here. I've never destroyed anyhar.'

'Fahn might contest that,' I said.

'Ysobi gets off on it, Jass. There's no getting away from it. He's messed with Gesaril's mind, as he messed with yours. The only difference is that you're a stronger har. Ag knows what he's saying to Gesaril. The har should have been sent back to the Shadowvales, you know that. Only he's still here. If you don't believe me...' He shook his head again. 'Nohar will speak to you about it, because they're scared you'll run, like Mori did. Although...' He fixed me with a stare. 'It hasn't got that bad yet. Don't let it, Jass, please.'

'What was so bad? Why did Mori run?'

It wasn't easy to listen to it. All the time, I visualised Mori having my face. It didn't help. The trouble started because the unnamed student needed Ysobi's full attention, or so he said to Mori. The har was damaged, fragile... It sounded all too familiar. The student was distressed by Ysobi's chesna bond with Mori; he felt jealous and inadequate. But, instead of simply saying 'Tough luck, I'm just your teacher. Don't

109

get fixated on me,' Ysobi asked Mori if, for a while, they could keep their bond low key, not obvious. Mori said to his friends that it was as if Ysobi had asked him to pretend their relationship didn't exist and never had. He was confused, wondering if he was at fault to mind about it. Listening to this narrative, my blood slowly froze in my veins. I swear I could feel the crystals forming. Like me, Mori had tried to be understanding and dispassionate, but it came to the point when he was seeing less and less of Ysobi, and hara were starting to look at him askance. Eventually, he confronted Ysobi. He asked why a student should make such demands, and suggested it wasn't exactly normal. In response, Ysobi accused him of being small-minded and jealous.

'Tell me, *is* that normal?' Zehn asked. 'Mori wasn't jealous. He was as accommodating as you're trying to be. He was in love, but despite that, he kept getting slapped – severely.'

'How did it end?'

Zehn sighed. 'It wasn't good.'

The worst thing about the situation was that Ysobi somehow undermined Mori so much, he began to think he was in the wrong. He waited for the tiniest crumbs of approval that Ysobi would throw from the table. Even listening to it, I felt sick. There were good days, after Ysobi had been pleasant with him, when Mori would seem at one with himself again, and then there were the bad days. The student, like Gesaril, was obsessed. He took to lurking round Mori's home and once a window was broken. Mori took to sleeping with a knife beneath his pillow because three times he woke up in the morning to find his house had been broken into and his possessions damaged. He was reluctant to tell Ysobi about this, since he thought Ysobi wouldn't believe him, and sure enough, when it finally got too much and Mori had to speak, Ysobi accused him of trying to hurt the student deliberately, of spreading gossip and lies. Of course, Mori had talked to hara about it. Who wouldn't?

'It was like a slow erosion of his spirit,' Zehn said. 'We told him to end the chesna bond, but he wouldn't listen to anyhar. He tortured himself about his supposed faults, questioning his own sanity, I think. It was as if he was completely under a spell. Ysobi sent him a letter, insisting it was out of concern, but listing everything Mori should and should not do in order to get along with others. It was just a list of complaints, nothing more. Mori took it all in and told hara he had a problem controlling himself. You felt like you wanted to slap him, or shake him out of it, but he was also worn so thin, it seemed cruel even to address it with him.'

'I don't understand,' I interrupted. 'Hara welcomed Yz into the social group with me. Why would they do that if he'd been so vile?'

Zehn shrugged. 'He's not dislikeable, Jass. And he is our highest-ranking hienama. A damn good one too. Everyhar blamed the student, said he'd fooled Ysobi. We all wanted to believe it, because to believe otherwise of a spiritual mentor kind of destroys the whole picture, doesn't it? I think Sinnar spoke to Ysobi about it, and what little information filtered through suggested Ysobi was in a mess too. He felt Mori was too demanding, too clingy. He couldn't deal with it. But Mori wasn't like that. Not really. The situation just ground him down. It would have been better if Ysobi could have just finished it, since Mori lacked the strength to, but he didn't. Sometimes, he was how he'd always been; affectionate and understanding. The next minute he was distant and harsh. You can imagine; it was slow torture for Mori. It got to the point where he felt Ysobi blamed him for everything, for existing, I guess. So one night, he simply upped and left. He disappeared, without a word to anyhar.'

'Didn't any of you go after him?'

Zehn nodded. 'Sinnar sent some hara, mainly because he was afraid Mori would do something bad to himself, but they tracked him down to Two Meadows and he told them to leave him alone. He didn't want to come back, not for anything. After that, I heard a few things about how something similar had happened a couple of times before. Ysobi doesn't socialise because of it, apparently. He says he knows what effect some aspects of the training can have and yet... well, now there's you. It's as if he can only resist for so long.'

I felt as if I'd been beaten up and rubbed both hands over my face, very hard, as if to press away the unwelcome truth. 'And yet you all let me...' I shouldn't have said it, but it was a thought expressed aloud. 'You all *let* me.'

'Well... despite me... most hara thought it *was* different this time. And maybe it is, because he's doing it behind your back. It's probably because of the harling.'

'His name is Zeph,' I said.

'Don't leave here,' Zehn said.

'I have no intention of doing so.' A surge of pure anger poured through me. 'You want it to go bad between Yz and me, I know you do. Forget it, Zehn. What you want: it's never going to happen. You can tell me tales all you want. It's the past. I won't judge the present by other hara's experiences. Now, will you let me go?'

He'd held on to me all that time. I had pins and needles in one arm.

'Don't be a fool,' Zehn said. 'At least investigate. I'm not lying to you.'

I investigated all right. I went back into the bar and took Zeph from Fahn's arms. Minnow dashed over to me and said, 'What did he tell you?'

'Nothing,' I said. 'I'm going now. See you later.'

'We're your friends,' Minnow said.

'Are you?' I walked out.

Whatever Zehn had said, and however much I thought it was coloured by his own desires, Minnow's simple words had confirmed Zehn's information. I went straight to Sinnar's house.

I knew my way around and snuck around the guest wing until I found the occupied room. Nohar saw me, or maybe they *had* seen me approach and gave me the space I needed.

Gesaril was alone. I was thankful for that, because I'm not sure what I would have done if Ysobi had been with him. The har looked dreadful, a shadow. I stood over his bed, with Zeph held against me. I stared down at him, projecting the dehara know what. He woke from a fretful sleep and saw me there. He didn't speak.

'Tell me,' I said coldly, 'what is it you want, Gesaril?'

'Only him,' he answered simply, rawly, as if every last shred of strength had been wrung from him. 'I'm sorry.'

Was he?

'You can kill me,' he said. 'I can't put up a fight.'

'You should go home.'

'He won't let me.' Gesaril stared at Zeph, and I saw then he was not the har he'd been when he'd first arrived. All that flirty madness of youth had gone. He was hollow, as a dead tree is hollow.

Zeph was very still against me, although I could hear him breathing. Maybe I shouldn't have brought him to this place. 'You want to go home, Gesaril?' I asked. My lips were numb, but somehow I could speak.

Gesaril stared at me with dull eyes. 'I don't know. I don't know anything.'

'If you want to go home, I will arrange it. If you don't, well...' I shrugged. 'Gesaril, you do understand the arrangement between Ysobi and I, don't you?'

'He had a harling with you,' Gesaril said. 'He said he'd always wanted to try, see if he could do it. But...'

'There is no but,' I said. 'He is the father of this harling. He has responsibilities. I can't let you have him, Gesaril. You should know: you are not the first.'

'And neither are you,' he said, a spark coming into his eyes. Then he sighed and turned his head to the side on the pillow. 'I wish I hadn't come here.'

A sentiment I shared. 'You're sick. You should be at home. Ysobi is not the right teacher for you.'

'He is,' Gesaril said, raising himself on his elbows.

His voice sounded feverish. 'He is. When I'm with him, I'm whole. He says I'll get better.'

There were some things I had to know. I realised that Gesaril might well lie to me, but I just wanted to see his face as he answered me, hoping I had enough intuition to know the truth. 'Gesaril, what exactly have you been led to believe the future holds for you with Ysobi?'

'He'll never forsake me,' Gesaril said. 'He told me that. He holds me in his arms at night and tells me that. He kisses my hair. It's meant to be. You're being cruel, holding that harling over him. He wants to be free, can't you see?'

'You're hardly more than a child,' I said. 'You know nothing, Gesaril. You sought to ensnare Ysobi, and you were clever about it. He can't resist you, maybe, but it's the challenge of you he's attracted to, nothing else. If I left Jesith tomorrow and never came back, do you really think you could keep him? Don't fool yourself. I have too many friends here. Your life would be a misery and eventually there'd be another student. Trust me, I know. I know the way it is, and I'm old enough to cope with it. You wouldn't have a chance.'

Gesaril flopped back on the bed, staring at the ceiling. His throat convulsed. 'I can't fight you, Jassenah, but when he knows you've been here, you'll be sorry.'

I laughed spitefully. 'Oh, my dear harling, that is not the case. Look at you. Look at me. If you want to drown, then do so. I'll watch from the edge of the bottomless pool. I have great patience. But think on this: When you are with him, then I am there too.

Don't ever doubt it. I'll always be with you, Gesaril. You'll feel me around, trust me.'

He stared at me, and I stared back. I fancied I saw in his eyes a slight shift, as if he was recalling sending bad thoughts my way.

I smiled sweetly. 'That's all I have to say to you. Return to your troubled dreams. Sleep well.'

With these words, I left him.

I was numb, inside and out. Half of what I'd said I hadn't meant and yet at the time when I'd stood by Gesaril's bed I'd been somehar else, somehar far more vengeful than I normally was.

I walked back to town, full of conflicting plans, and Zeph whispered mournfully in my ear, 'Jassy, don't.' But I couldn't respond to him. I could feel his fear, however; the closest I'd come to mind touch with him.

'I'm sorry, Zeph,' I said, 'but I've got some business to attend to, and I need the space to do it. Where would you like to stay: Fahn's or Minnow and Vole's?'

He didn't answer at first. Then said, 'Fahn's.'

I went home first and put some stuff into a bag for Zeph. I didn't know what I was doing, but I was aware that Zeph shouldn't be around me at that time. Zeph sat on top of my bed and watched me with grave eyes. 'That har in the bed at Sinnar's is bad,' he said.

'I know. Don't worry. Everything will be OK.'

I drank some wine and, while Zeph dozed on the sofa, waited in the darkness for when I thought the band would finish at the Pool. I wasn't expecting Ysobi that night. I guess I knew where he'd be now. I couldn't believe he'd done this to me. It seemed such a grubby, shallow thing to do; so *human*. I felt disgusted, hurt, betrayed and furious. If he'd wanted that har so much, he should have told me. I'd given him the chance, for Ag's sake. And yet why did he want Gesaril? The har was a mess. He was barely even attractive now.

I watched the old clock that ticked away obliviously above the hearth in my sitting room. It had seen so many ages, that clock. It had ticked for the human family that had once lived here. I wondered how they'd ended and if the clock had just kept ticking all the way through.

Around 3 a.m., I left the house and went to Fahn's place. If he wasn't there, I'd wait for him. Maybe. Or maybe I'd go to Minnow's. I didn't know what to do. I didn't know what I was planning even. But there was a light in Fahn's kitchen. I looked through the window, Zeph in my arms, and saw Fahn had a few friends back. They were drinking, laughing, talking loudly. Too happy. I projected a mind touch in the hope Fahn would hear me. He turned almost at once, and without saying anything to his friends, came outside. He dragged me away from the window.

'Jass,' he said, then shook his head. I knew he wanted to embrace me, because Fahn was a great one for physical contact, but he could tell my skin was on fire and he might get burned if he tried it.

'Will you look after Zeph for me for a while?' I said crisply.

He stared at me. 'If that's what you want.'

'It is. Look, you've probably guessed, but Zehn has told me... certain things. I need some space to think about it.'

'You think I'm a bad friend now, right, because I didn't tell you?' Fahn looked very pale in the starlight, his arms folded defensively.

'No. Zehn explained. It doesn't matter. I'm the fool, not you, nor any of the others. Here.' I handed Zeph to him, who was uncharacteristically silent. He clung to Fahn at once and buried his face in the har's luxurious red mane.

'It might not be what you think,' Fahn said. 'We might all be wrong.'

'That might be so,' I said.

'But if you want any help beating the crap out of that Shadowvales scum, you know where to come.'

I smiled. 'Yeah. Thanks, Fahn. In a way, I saw it coming.'

I kissed the back of Zeph's head. He would not look at me. A pang of guilt slipped through me, but I couldn't think of his feelings now. My future was hanging in the balance; both our futures.

I just walked into the night. As I walked, I thought about how female I'd become; something that at the start of my Wraeththu life, I couldn't believe would ever happen. I'd always appreciated I had the female parts, which I'd viewed as eminently useful and pleasurable, but in some ways I'd looked upon myself as simply a modified male. Now I realised I had the female psyche too. I thought differently. We all did. I imagined that I felt like all the betrayed wives and mothers of the old human world had felt. It was interesting, this perspective. As a human, I'd often been violent, but it had been a brute animal thing, without reason. The violence inside me now was focused, like an arrow. If I unleashed it, it would go straight to the heart. No flailing limbs, no coarse cries. It was far more devastating. I knew the wiles of women, now; knew them through and through. It was astounding to discover that in so many ways they'd been the stronger sex. If the boy I'd once been had ever guessed he'd turn out like this, he would probably have drowned himself. But the fact was, I didn't care about it. I was glad. I felt very alive in that vibrant spring night. My pain was like fireworks, filling up the sky with light.

Just before dawn, I found myself at Zehn's doorstep. Even as I knocked on his door, I knew this was probably the wrong thing to do, but the fact was I needed comfort. Zehn loved me and desired me. He would be full of righteous anger on my behalf. He would hold me and say things I wanted to hear.

I had to knock several times before I roused him and then I realised he probably wasn't alone. He came to the door, opened it and stood staring at me for some seconds. His face was utterly without expression, his hair mussed from sleep, or passion, or both.

'Here I am,' I said, in an arch voice.

He lowered his head and appraised me from beneath his brows. 'Are you here to rip my head off?'

'No. I'm here to let you enjoy saying "I told you so." Can I come in?'

He hesitated a moment, then nodded. 'Yes, of course.'

I went into his kitchen, which was as disorderly as I'd imagined it would be. There were empty bottles on the table, two stone goblets. 'Is Arken here?'

'Mmm.' Zehn cleared a space for me to sit down,

since every chair was covered in clothes, crocks, bits of horse tackle, and other junk. 'What did you do last night?'

'I investigated, as you suggested.'

He sat down opposite me and folded his arms on the table. 'And?'

'You were right,' I said. 'I have to think what to do next, and wanted to talk to you. Do you mind?'

He shook his head slowly. I think he did mind, actually. Could I blame him? I'd run to him as a last resort. It was insulting.

I sighed and ran my fingers through my hair. 'It's OK. This was a bad move. I'll go.' I stood up.

'No,' he said. 'Don't. I'll make some coffee.' He went to the narrow stairs and yelled, 'Ark!'

Arken appeared shortly afterwards. When he saw me, I could see he wasn't pleased, not because of anything to do with Zehn and me, but because I was an emotional casualty and he wasn't sure what to say.

'Excuse me for being here,' I said to him. 'I won't stay long.'

'Are you... um... all right?' Arken asked.

'Fairly.'

He went to Zehn and put his arms around him. 'I'll head off, don't worry.'

'You don't have to go,' I said.

'I think I do,' he said. 'Talk with Zehn. It's no problem.'

After Arken had left, Zehn and I did not talk. He made some cursory attempt to clear up and made the coffee. Then we sat in silence at the table, sipping drinks that were too hot. Eventually, Zehn sighed and put down his mug. 'Why are you here, Jass?'

'I don't know. I just found myself here. I've been walking around all night.'

'Did you find them together?'

'No. I talked to the little shit, though. I'm not Mori, Zehn. I'm not going to fall apart. However, I've yet to decide whether I can stay here.'

'You should get away for a couple of days maybe,' Zehn said.

I laughed harshly. 'Like where?'

'Shadowvales. I know the little shit comes from there, but it's a tranquil place and it's close. It'd be good for you.'

'I don't know anyhar there though. I'm not sure I want to be alone.' I rubbed my hair again. 'Hell, I don't know what to do.'

'I'll take you to the Shadowvales,' Zehn said. 'If you want to go.'

I stared at him for a few moments. 'You don't have to do that.'

'Of course I don't, but I will.'

'That's good of you. Thanks.'

'I said I was your friend, and I meant it. Despite appearances, I think it's right you came to me. I'm just not entirely sure how I feel about it. You know what I want to say to you, and I'm sure you suspect my motives.'

'You think I should finish it, of course. Don't worry. I doubt you'll be alone with that advice.'

'It's difficult for me to advise you because of how much I feel for you.' It was the first time he'd actually admitted it so openly. 'I'm not unbiased. Some hara will think badly of me if I go away with you.'

'Like Arken?'

Zehn laughed softly. 'No, not him. He's the first har I've ever been truly honest with, I think. He knows all about you.'

'I see...'

'So, before we do anything else, I have to say certain things, get them off my chest.'

'All right.'

He took a deep breath. 'I could kill him for what he's done to you. He's so fucking privileged. He has what I want, and he treats it as nothing. I don't want to hear anything remotely flattering about him, or any justifications you might want to concoct for him. I don't even want to hear or speak his name. He's a prize-winning shit, an arrogant fuck and totally stupid. I would never treat you that way, ever.'

'I know,' I said. 'I know you'd never treat me that way.'

'And I can never have you, not like he has you. I know that. You'll probably take aruna with me some time in the near future, because you'll need the closeness, and I'll take what I can get. I think you're fond of me, but it'll never be like what you feel for that... Anyway, I just had to say it.'

'I know.'

'Don't patronise me, Jass.'

'I'm not. I don't know what else to say.'

'Do you still love him?'

'I don't know. It's impossible to tell. At the moment, I could cheerfully hang him from the nearest oak.'

Zehn grinned. 'I have a rope.'

I didn't tell anyhar where I was going. I knew Zeph

would be fine with Fahn. Let them all wonder what had happened to me. Let them all put two and two together when Arken told them I'd visited Zehn and they noticed Zehn was missing too. Why I felt I should punish my friends instead of the one har who truly deserved it, I have no idea. Ysobi would no doubt be unconcerned about my disappearance. He might even feel relief. I knew I was in a dangerous situation. It would be so easy to fall into Zehn's arms, and give him what he wanted. But that wouldn't be fair. Not really. Because I wanted Ysobi to be jealous. I wanted him to realise he wanted me.

The Shadowvales is a beautiful location, hidden in a deep cove, its buildings huddled against the black cliffs. The hara there were mystical and serene. I found it hard to imagine them having emotional crises. Zehn and I took a room, which fortunately we could pay for with sins (I never tire of the humorous aspect of those words), in a sway-backed old inn, run by three hara who looked as if they belonged in a medieval fantasy of wayward fairy folk. It took us only two hours to ride there from Jesith, so we took lunch in a room that looked down into the narrow harbour. 'I think we're too human,' I said to Zehn.

'Why's that?'

'All this stupid mess. It's such a waste of time and energy. I don't know who's worse; me or him. Ysobi comes over as all über-har, but he was the one who wanted the harling. He was into the chesna fantasy more, I'm sure. I can't believe I fell for it. I can't believe I fell for him. I had a crush on my teacher. It was pitiable.'

'Much as I enjoy hearing this, you don't mean it,'

Zehn said. 'It's just your anger talking.'

'We shouldn't be like this, Zehn,' I said. 'It didn't work for humans and it won't work for us. We should just have roon friends and get on with life, not get screwed up with emotions and so on. I've learned my lesson.'

'I tried living like that,' Zehn said. 'Unfortunately, I was the only har I knew who felt it was a valid way of life.'

'Well, maybe I was wrong to criticise you. Fahn fell for you like I fell for Ysobi, like starry-eyed human teenagers. We should be ashamed of ourselves. I know you love me, Zehn, but you don't behave like I did, or Fahn, or even Ysobi. You're so... *measured.*'

'It's supposed to be me saying things to make *you* feel better,' Zehn said. 'Do shut up, Jass.'

'You see?' I gestured expansively. 'That's exactly what I mean.'

Zehn took my hands in his own over the table top. 'Hey... rant all you like. But think about what you're going to do.'

I squeezed his fingers. 'Do? I suppose the obvious answer is to go home after a few days, carry on with my job, bring up Zeph, see what life brings. I have a harling now, for the Ag's sake: a child! How the hell did I fall into this? I won't run, Zehn. But I'm bruised. I'm bruised really badly. I let him *into me.*'

'We'll help you,' Zehn said. 'All of us.'

'I know you will.' There was a silence. 'Shall we go for a walk? Show me around. Let's see if we can spot the little shit's relatives.'

We walked out to the old lighthouse, now dim, that

stood on the headland above the harbour. Here, Zehn took me in his arms and we shared breath. It was a friendly, non-demanding thing. I realised he was like a brother to me, but also more than that. He was not Ysobi, though. We sat on the bare rocks that were little islands in the scrub of coarse grass, and watched the sun go down. The tide was still going out, which was fortunate; otherwise we might have been stranded.

'It feels so ancient here,' I said. 'It's almost as if the land hasn't yet realised that things have changed, that we're here.'

Zehn lay back beside me, and stretched languorously. The image of his beauty was not lost on me. 'Things have changed a lot in just a few years,' he said. 'I think that if we went far beyond the phylarchy, most of what we knew in the old world would have gone.'

I nodded, hugging my knees. 'Do you ever wonder what happened to the human androgynes?'

Zehn pulled a quizzical face at me. 'What?'

'Well, the humans who were like us anyway, more or less. The ones that people called freaks, only they probably weren't at all. It wasn't uncommon, Zehn. Maybe they were precursors to us, dreams in the DNA. Were any of them incepted, do you think? I wonder about them, that's all.'

Zehn put his arms behind his head. 'I expect they're dancing on humanity's grave.'

'I hope so. The world was a bad place, a very bad place. I want it to be better now, and it has to start with the individual, doesn't it?'

He smiled at me. 'I like the way you sound strong

now.'

I leaned back on straight arms, face raised to the sky. 'I feel good, surprisingly. I feel washed clean. I feel like I'm about to make a breakthrough.'

Zehn reached up and took a lock of my hair in his fingers, held it to his nose. I could feel his breath in every strand. We were magical creatures.

'Zehn,' I said. I lay down beside him and we shared breath again. He was so cautious, wanting me desperately yet having to battle with a sensible part of his mind that was shouting 'No!'

Eventually, he drew away from me. 'Let's go to a fish restaurant. The Shadowvales is renowned for them. Let's dine like kings and then go to bed. If you wish, I can attempt to take you to realms undreamed of, or we can just sleep. Your choice.'

I laughed. 'Let's just start with the food.'

We drank a lot of the local ale with the meal, which had the effect of loosening my tongue. I told Zehn my suspicions that Gesaril might have tried to attack me psychically. I also told him about my majhahn with Sinnar. 'He thought the same,' I said. 'I wasn't imagining it. I know you don't want justifications for He Who Must Not Be Named At The Moment, but I wonder whether the little shit's been screwing with our minds magically.'

Zehn rolled his eyes. 'Oh, come off it, Jass. He's hardly more than a harling. How could he have such power? Even if he could affect you, which I doubt, there's no way he could affect His Eminence, the Fuckwit.'

'I want to believe that,' I said. 'I really do, but the

emotions of the young can be very intense. Maybe that's enough of a battery to provide the power.'

Zehn considered my words, ducked his head. 'There is that, I suppose.' He grinned. 'Then fight fire with fire. Smite the little shit!'

I was silent for a moment. 'Would you do majhahn with me?'

He watched me carefully and did not smile. 'No,' he said. 'I was joking.'

'No you weren't. Just for a moment, you weren't.'

Zehn took my hands. 'I don't think you should do anything like that. If Fuckwit wants the little shit, I think you should let them have each other. Be bigger than that, Jass.' He squeezed my fingers. 'Please.'

I sighed through my nose, dropped my head. 'OK.'

We left the restaurant and walked out into the spicy cold of a Shadowvales spring night. We walked beyond the harbour and listened to the clean white waves smashing against the ancient rocks. We held hands, and I was filled with a wistful kind of melancholy. The sea went on forever. It was the most beautiful thing; primal and powerful.

Around midnight, we ambled back to our inn room. Zehn bought a flagon of heather wine from the bar, which was just closing. When we'd arrived, we'd taken only one room, because despite nothing being said, we'd both taken it for granted we would not sleep separately that night. Like Zehn, I was in two minds, but the combination of grief, ale, wine and the simple need for aruna shouldered aside all sensible caution. We sat in the dark, drinking the wine and talking amiably the unfettered gibberish of the drunken. The innkeepers had thoughtfully lit a fire in our room, so the darkness was tinged with warm hues.

At one point, Zehn took my wine cup off me and pressed me back on the bed to share breath. His mouth was warm and relaxed and smelled of wine. He put a hand inside my shirt. It occurred to me then that I hadn't been soume since Zeph's pearl had dropped. Letting Zehn be the first seemed a significant act, something that properly belonged to Ysobi. He wanted to be ouana anyway, no doubt because of what had happened between us before, so the issue wasn't discussed. I took his hand and guided him to the place where he'd realise I was eager for him. He uttered a soft gasp in pleasure, caressed me. Zehn didn't give a damn about sikras or focused aruna. He wanted to take my mind and body on a wild intoxicating ride, that's all. We virtually ripped off each other's clothes and I pulled him onto me. When he pushed inside me, it hurt a bit, as if I was new from inception. It was as if my soume-lam had remade itself to be new. I kept saying his name aloud until he put his mouth over my own. Then I kept saying it in my mind, like a shout.

We spent several days indulging our senses, which meant we rose from our bed only to go out and sample the different restaurants in the town. The bed made a hideous racket – creaks, groans, squeaks and a mystifying clanking sound – whenever we took aruna in it, which led our kindly hosts to make gentle jokes whenever we appeared, bedraggled and languorous, for our brief periods of refuelling. They must have thought we were celebrating a recent chesna bond majhahn or something, because once while we were out they put red flowers in our room and another time left us a sachet of herbal cream that could be used to heighten pleasure.

I wanted aruna to grant me oblivion, to make me not care, and in some ways it did that. But on the third night, I felt restless. Zehn was asleep beside me, while I sat up in the bed, not in the least bit tired. I mulled over recent events, like picking at the edges of a healing wound. I imagined that Ysobi was with Gesaril now and their cries of release winged round my mind like mad birds. I wanted to appear at their bedside and stab them both to death. Of course, I'd been drinking that night, and I hope that was largely what impelled me to creep from the bed and pull on my clothes.

I went down to the sea and stood upon the sand. The air was bitterly cold, but the night was clear and a waning moon hung heavy in the sky, not long past full. The waves seemed alive like elemental beasts, prancing upon the shore. The tide was slowly creeping back to the land, devouring all in its path. Without really thinking about what I was doing, I created an etheric Nayati in my head and marked its boundaries. I raised my arms, and with my hair whipping around my face, I yelled into the wind, calling upon Aruhani. I visualised him hanging before me, his face expressionless, although I knew he was listening. 'Avenge me,' I said. 'You are the divine hostling of my son, as I am the earthly hostling. Protect us and remove all evil influence from our lives. Let those who have stood against me receive all due reward. Let it be quick, Devourer, let it be direct.'

I collapsed onto my knees in the sand, my hair

hanging around me like a ripped shawl. It was done.

Zehn and I rode back to Jesith in the early morning, a ground mist hugging our horses' feet. He hadn't known I'd left our room last night, and I didn't tell him. All I'd said to him when we awoke was, 'We have to go back to Jesith now, Zehn.'

On the journey home, Zehn didn't say much, and I sensed he felt sad our short escape was over. I wasn't sure what I felt; it was a complex mix. On the one hand, I was uncomfortable with the thought of having to deal with things – not least the fact I'd abandoned Zeph for three days and had been absent from my work. I was troubled about what I'd done on the beach the previous night; in daylight it seemed unwise at best. The thought of Ysobi was another matter. If I thought of his face, a thrill went through me that was part anger, part longing. I wanted to speak to him and yet also to give him the full force of my disdain. I had reached a nexus point. How I dealt with this personal situation would set the course of my life as a har. Aruhani would know I'd acted from pain; there would be no smiting. I must strive not to repeat outdated human patterns. I must rise above the situation and look down on it objectively.

At the outskirts of Jesith, Zehn pulled his mount to a halt. 'I'm going to leave you here,' he said. 'I'll go and report at the forest waypoint, and hope I don't get too much of a beating for skiving off.'

'Thanks, Zehn,' I said. I leaned over to kiss him, perhaps thinking we could share breath for a last time, but he guided his horse away.

'No, Jass. I'll see you later.' He kicked the animal

and it cantered off towards the trees.

For some moments, I just stayed where I was. I had a feeling I was going to have to face trouble of several sorts.

First, I went to Fahn's, who was at home. I thought this was probably because he'd been landed with a harling to care for. He seemed relieved to see me, but there was an edge to his voice. 'Where have you been? A lot of hara thought you and Zehn had run off together, but then...' he shrugged, '... I was going to say I didn't think you'd just leave Zeph behind, but I'm not even sure I'm right about that.'

'How's he been?' I asked. 'I'm sorry, Fahn, and I'm grateful for what you've done. I just needed time to think.'

'*Think?*' Fahn gave me a sour glance, which reminded me of the feelings he'd once had for Zehn.

'Yes. Think. I'll take Zeph off your hands now. Is he angry with me?'

'Confused, really. He sensed something going on, without really understanding it. He kept saying you'd be back. He had more faith than most of us.'

'Where is he?'

Fahn looked troubled. 'You can't take him, Jass, because Ysobi came for him two days ago.'

'What? And you just handed him over?'

'He *is* Zeph's father. How could I refuse?'

I sighed deeply. 'What did he say?'

'Nothing much. He was looking for Zeph, maybe for you too. I had to say the harling was here and he just took him.' Fahn drew a breath. 'Jass, this is a small community and we're all supposed to work together. Sinnar isn't pleased about this situation, not any of it. I think you should go and see him right away.'

I rode fast to the vineyard, with a hideous spiralling feeling inside me as if everything was way beyond my control. Hara in the yard, who were loading an order onto a cart, gave me a guarded greeting. One of them said, 'Sinnar's in his office.'

I went there directly.

Sinnar is typically a laid back individual, who is hard to ruffle. He wasn't ruffled that day either, but he didn't greet me with his usual open smile. He looked tense; there was a line between his brows. 'I'm glad you've decided to return,' he said brusquely.

'I'm really sorry,' I said.

'Good. Sit down.'

I did so, feeling utterly chastised.

Sinnar regarded me thoughtfully for some moments, hands folded on his desk. 'You should have at least come to me and told me you needed time away. I run a business, Jass, and it's the lifeblood of this community. You left tasks half-finished. It was inconsiderate of you just to take off like that. Also, I don't think it was right that you just dumped your son on Fahn. You're an adult. You have responsibilities now, much as you and Zehn might want to keep play-acting at being reckless young hara, still bleeding from inception.'

I displayed my hands. 'I'm sorry.'

'You can say that as many times as you like, but I just want you to think about it.' He softened. 'I know you're having a hard time, and that you went to our home to see Gesaril. Was that what made you run?'

I nodded. 'Yes. Sort of. Don't blame Zehn. He was trying to help me sort my head out.'

Sinnar grunted vaguely. 'Have you spoken to Ysobi yet?'

I shook my head. 'No. He took Zeph from Fahn's house.'

'I know. I advised him to. The harling shouldn't suffer because his parents can't act like grown-ups.'

I looked at Sinnar in appeal. 'I don't know whether Ysobi even wants to see me. I don't know what to think.'

'I'll summon him here,' Sinnar said. 'You should confront one another. This situation is more serious than you think, but I won't speak about it until Ysobi is here too. I doubt he'd want you to hear what I've got to say, but to be honest I don't care if it embarrasses him. Things have gone on long enough.'

It was the closest I'd ever seen Sinnar get to being angry.

When Ysobi walked into that office, he was like a stranger wearing a familiar face. He looked gorgeous, though. It hurt me to see him. He wouldn't meet my eyes beyond an initial curt greeting and a nod of the head. I got the impression he was mortified rather than hostile. Ysobi had always seemed so in control of himself, but that day he was almost like an abashed child. Sinnar bade Ysobi sit in a chair beside me, and stared at us both. Uncomfortable silence stretched out. Ysobi cleared his throat, crossed his legs. I was puzzled that he didn't speak.

'Well,' Sinnar said. 'Something intrigues me. Tell me, do you two know what a chesna bond constitutes?'

'Yes,' I said.

Ysobi said softly, exasperatedly, 'For Ag's sake, Sin.'

'Yes, for the Aghama's sake,' Sinnar said firmly. 'Come on, tell me – at least one of you. I want to hear it.'

Ysobi just stared at Sinnar, with something like challenge in his eyes.

I spoke just to break the silence. 'It's when two hara want to share their life together, unconditionally.'

'Is that so?' Sinnar said. 'So tell me, what does unconditionally mean?'

'It means,' Ysobi said in a rather insulting drawl, 'that the relationship simply exists as an entity, but there are no demands made by either party, just serene acceptance of the common feeling. It is a union beyond jealousy and insecurity and the need to possess.'

I sensed criticism in those words. 'That's exactly what it is,' I said, turning in my chair to face him, 'but it's also honesty and respect.'

Ysobi gave me a hard glance. It transfixed me.

'It's all of those things,' Sinnar said. 'It's Wraeththu's way of honouring true love, for want of a less sentimental term. We have striven to overcome human weakness, but to be frank all I've seen recently is like something from my old human life. My parents behaved like you did. It saddens me.'

'Sinnar, it seems to me we were wrong,' I said, turning away from Ysobi. 'What we had wasn't chesna. It was something else.'

'Jassenah!' Ysobi snapped. 'Don't talk like a

spoiled child.'

'Ysobi, stop *insulting* me,' I retorted.

'Both of you, shut up,' Sinnar said. 'I don't think Jass is entirely blameless in this situation, but the time has come for some painful truths to be spoken, Yz. I've sent word to Kyme for your mentor to come here.'

'What?' Ysobi said. 'Why?'

'Because it's clear to me you need his guidance. I don't want to lose you, because you're valuable to our community, but I can't tolerate your... *indiscretions* any longer.'

'What do you mean by that?' Ysobi asked icily.

'I mean that you seem to have an unhealthy addiction to certain behaviours. It's like I imagine a serial killer would be. They kill, then can manage for so long without killing, before the urge takes them again.'

Ysobi laughed. 'You can't be serious!'

'I am very serious. On the one hand, you obviously want a chesna bond with somehar, but on the other you do all in your power to destroy it once you have it. You have an unsavoury tendency to seduce your students in a manner that leaves them vulnerable...'

Ysobi stood up. 'I won't listen to this. Are you mad? All I do is care for those who need my care. I've made the mistake of trying to have chesna relationships with hara I love – and believe me, I loved all of them – but now I realise it's impossible. There are no hara removed enough from their humanity to properly understand what a chesna bond should be.'

Sinnar's voice was low in comparison to Ysobi's

heated remarks. He folded his hands before him. 'You have to listen to me, Yz. Sit down!'

Ysobi hesitated, then did so.

'I am phylarch of this community,' Sinnar said, 'and its welfare comes before all other considerations. You have a good reputation, which means that Jesith has a good reputation. If you insist on destroying that, it reflects on everyhar else. These dramatic episodes are ridiculous. Once could have been an accident, twice a mistake, but three times?' Sinnar shook his head. 'It has to stop, or you will no longer operate from our Nayati.'

'Are you firing me?'

'No, not yet. I'm fond of you. I want you to realise there's a problem and then sort it out.'

'My private life is my business,' Ysobi said coldly. 'You have no right to lecture me on it, or have I misunderstood the role of the phylarch in our community?'

'It is your business, yes,' Sinnar answered mildly, 'but when it affects the community as a whole it becomes mine also. Gesaril should be sent home, but do you really think we could send him back to his family at the moment? He'll tell them everything, and if not them, then somehar else. He came to us as a healthy young har and now he's a demented neurotic! So much for your "first-class training." Just how will that look? What in the Aghama's name was in your head while you were sneaking into my house to take aruna with him?'

'I did not sneak into your house,' Ysobi said. 'Neither did I visit him for the purpose you suggested. Don't cheapen my calling, Sinnar. I have a responsibility to Gesaril, which everyhar in Jesith seems to want me to ignore. I can't help the way he feels about me, but I do feel responsible for helping him get over it.'

'Maybe you should stop acting like a high-class whore during training, then,' I said.

Both hara gawped at me in surprise.

I shrugged. 'Well, it was the arunic arts that contributed to me falling for Ysobi in the first place. I'd never experienced anything like it. I'm not surprised others have been affected like I was.' I turned to face Ysobi again. 'You once said I seduced you. Well... if I did, it was because you wanted me to, I think. There's a depth to what you do that transcends mere training, Yz. It's a deep connection. I don't think you're academic about it at all, really. Not every hienama offers that kind of training. It's your speciality. You're known for it. Hara pay you to come and get it.' I gestured with both hands. 'So what does that make you? What does that make them?'

'Do Orphie and Aeron come into that category?' he asked me, deadpan.

'No. You don't fancy *them*, do you?'

I glanced at Sinnar and saw that he was attempting to smother a smile. When he caught me looking at him, he straightened his face.

'All I ever did was love you,' Ysobi said, 'and you repaid me with suspicion and savagery.'

'All I ever did was love you,' I countered, 'and you repaid me with betrayal. A chesna bond is supposed to be unassailable. We should be able to be intimate with any number of hara and it shouldn't affect our relationship, but I knew Gesaril was a threat from the start. And as soon as I saw him, I knew *you* would be a liability.' I sighed. 'Why *did* you want him so much? Was it worth it? Was he so wonderful he eclipsed me in your eyes? We were so content before he came here. I just don't understand.'

'I am not in love with Gesaril,' Ysobi said. 'I've tried to explain to you dozens of times the way it is, and all I get is this possessive crap.'

'I'm *not*... Oh, fuck it!' I pressed my hands against my eyes briefly. 'What's the point? We can't understand each other's views. We might as well just decide what's to be done with Zeph and get it all over with.'

'I'll tell you what you'll do,' Sinnar said.

Ysobi and I both turned to him.

'Jass, you'll visit Gesaril and apologise for the curse he believes you've put on him. Or rather, you'll tell him it wasn't a curse.'

I felt myself colour up. 'What? Why does he think that?'

'He said you cursed him when you visited his bedside. You should make it clear to him you didn't... supposing that you didn't! He told me what you said. You should take it back.'

I stared at my hands. 'After what he said to me? I don't suppose he told you *that*. Do you really expect me to make him feel better?'

Sinnar was firm in his response. 'Yes, because he's young and unhinged, and you're not. It was Ysobi you should have confronted, not Gesaril. You are twice the har he is, and you terrified him. We have to attempt some damage limitation here. Ysobi, you will tell Gesaril that you can no longer be involved in his caste training, that you have become too personally concerned. You will also apologise to him. When Codexia Huriel arrives from Kyme, you will ask him to help you, Yz. I hope he can help Gesaril also.' Ysobi tried to say something, but Sinnar silenced him. 'Say nothing. This is the way it will be. You need to talk to Huriel about the problems you've been having. Aruna is not just sex, it's a potent force, and I really don't think hara yet appreciate the extent of its power. You need to control this "effect" you have on the impressionable. We can't risk anything like this happening again. Do you understand me?'

'You have no idea,' Ysobi said, then shook his head. 'I'm sorry, Sinnar, but you really don't know what you're talking about.'

'Maybe I don't,' Sinnar said. 'You're the hienama, not me. I'm just the har who has to keep things running smoothly in this town, and unfortunately for you, my word is law. As I said, I don't want to lose you, not least because you're a good friend. But if you can't see there's a problem, I don't know how we can proceed. In some ways, this is partly my fault. I should have addressed the situation with you after Morien.'

Ysobi stood up again. 'I have to go now, Sinnar. I'll speak to you again later.' He glanced at me. 'Zeph is with me, Jass.'

'I know,' I said. 'Do you want me to fetch him?'

'No. He's my son too. Come and see him, if you want to.' With these words, he walked out. Sinnar didn't try to stop him.

I sat there for some moments, dazed. It hadn't gone particularly well, I thought. I hadn't been lofty and objective enough.

Sinnar sighed and stretched. He rolled his head around and rubbed the back of his neck. 'I could do without all this,' he said.

'I *am* really sorry.'

'It's Zeph I worry about. Jass, what *do* you want?'

'The truth?' I laughed coldly. 'A rewind of time. Despite everything, I love that har. I must be mad.'

Sinnar's voice was gentler now. 'Then go and see him, talk to him. Let the dust settle a little, but when you go to him, don't argue. Remember what was said about chesna. I don't think you were wrong to be close to him. I think your bond was real. He just has a warped sense of duty to his students, and yes, I think you might have hit on a partial truth with what you said about his training methods. You ran, but you came back. This is your home and you're an asset to our community. Don't throw everything away without trying to salvage what's precious.'

'You're a wise har,' I said. 'Jesith is lucky to have you.'

'Wise?' Sinnar laughed. 'Not that. I just look for the easiest and cleanest ways out of trouble.'

'I'll go and see Gesaril. But not yet, OK?'

'Don't leave it too long,' Sinnar said, 'any of it. If you do, it might be too late to act.'

I stood up. 'I understand.' I ducked my head. 'Thank you.'

For another couple of days, I kept my distance from both Ysobi and Gesaril. Fahn was still rather frosty with me, and Orphie also kept away, which made me sad. Minnow and Vole were fine, even if there were some uncomfortable moments when I first saw them again. I asked Minnow to bring Zeph from the Nayati to spend time with me. I couldn't face Ysobi yet.

Zeph was clearly upset and my heart contracted. 'When can we come home?' he asked in a small mournful voice and it brought tears to my eyes.

'I don't know,' I said. 'I'm sorry, Zeph, but...'

How to tell a harling his parents had reached a cold bitter place? It was so wrong, so *human*, as Sinnar had pointed out.

'You should go and see Ysobi,' Minnow said to me.

'He could have come here,' I countered. 'He hasn't.'

Minnow rolled his eyes. 'Look, one of you has to bludgeon down the pride!'

I knew he was right, but I didn't want it to be me. I wanted Ysobi to come to me, to tell me he loved me best of all. I might snarl at him in reply, but I wouldn't know what I really felt until I heard him say he cared for me truly. My head was in a constant spin, knowing he was so close and yet so far.

I also kept away from Zehn, not least because late at night I wanted to go to his bed for comfort, which I knew was unfair. I did send him a gift, which was a bunch of red tulips, bound with ribbon and attached with a note that said, 'It's not the season for forget-me-nots, but these flowers are the colour of the passion you gave to me. Our time together will be with me always.'

He sent no responding note. It would take weeks before we could spend time in each other's company again.

Every time I went to work and bumped into

Sinnar, I was conscious of not having done the things he wanted me to do. On the afternoon of the second day, I gave in and went to his office. 'Can I have an hour or so off, please?'

He studied me. 'For?'

'Unfinished business,' I said.

Sinnar nodded and went back to his paperwork. 'Take the rest of the day off.'

Gesaril was out in the garden when I arrived at Sinnar's house. He was kneeling in the soil, tidying up the plants, pulling out last year's dead wood. He was so deep in thought he didn't hear me approach and only became aware of my presence when he sensed me looming behind him. His astonished jump was comical.

'Hello, Gesaril,' I said. 'Sinnar has asked me to come and tell you I haven't cursed you.'

Gesaril's face flushed. He turned back to his task and didn't say anything.

'Lost your tongue?' I enquired. 'You were fairly full of things you wanted to say a few nights ago.'

'I shouldn't have said anything,' he said. 'Please go.'

'Sorry, I can't. I made a promise. Do you really think you're cursed?'

He glanced at me. 'You know that I am.'

'If I did that, I lift it here and now,' I said.

He ignored me.

'Look,' I said, then sighed. 'Gesaril, what happened was not just your fault, and it was wrong of me to have confronted you that way. I was angry. You might have done the same in my position.'

He stopped what he was doing then and watched me warily, perhaps wondering whether this apparent pleasant front concealed weapons.

I hunkered down in front of him. 'Will you tell me the truth?'

'About what?'

'You and Ysobi.'

He nodded, frowning, not meeting my eyes. 'What do you want to know?'

'That time, when he began the arunic arts with you – did he really hurt you?'

He glanced at me then, quickly, then away. 'I should have told him,' he said, 'but I couldn't.'

'Told him what?'

Gesaril shook his head, half-heartedly pulled a dead stalk from the ground. 'I know about Orphie,' he said, which could have meant anything.

I shrugged, gestured with both hands, hoping he'd go on.

'Bad things happen,' he said. 'I think the towns we live in are bubbles. They're like dreams in bubbles. Outside, it's different.'

My thighs were aching, so I sat down. 'Are you talking about what happened to Orphie's hostling?' My voice was slightly sharp, because as far as I knew there was only one har who could tell him such a thing, and it certainly wasn't Orphie. The only har I'd told was Ysobi.

Gesaril nodded again, still unable to meet my eyes. 'There were five of us. We thought we were safe. Everyhar thought we were safe, because the Shadowvales is a magical place. We were playing on the beach, some miles from town. They came in from the sea, that's all. Two of us got away.'

I stared at him. 'What are you saying?'

Gesaril's gaze was unfocused; he looked right through me. 'I was five years old. My parents told me I'd forget, that I was har and therefore I'd heal properly, through and through.' He fixed me with his eyes. 'Sometimes, I see those creatures in the fields. I can't be sure it's not real. I heard about Orphie. These things happen.'

He returned to his weeding. I stared at his back for some moments. My mouth had gone dry. 'Gesaril, are you saying that somehar committed pelki on you when you were a harling?'

He nodded, but didn't stop what he was doing. 'They were har, but they didn't look like it. They were insane. Animals. Full of hate. To them, harlings were loathsome.'

'Why didn't your hara tell any of us about this?'

'Because they think it's over, that I'm all right. That's the way things are in the Shadowvales. Bad things aren't allowed to exist. It's all serene.'

'Gesaril, look at me.'

He didn't for a few seconds, but then turned round.

'How did you get through feybraiha?'

He shrugged. 'My friend was with me. He was young, it wasn't too demanding. I like aruna, Jassenah. That's not the problem.'

'Then, what is?'

'If I'm careful, it's OK. If I'm ouana, it's OK. I usually am.' He laughed sadly. 'I can see what you're thinking. You've decided what kind of har I am. What was it you called me to your friends? A soume shrew?'

144

I wasn't pleased somehar had felt it necessary to tell him that. 'Well...'

'It doesn't matter. I know what I'm like. It's like a shout to the world to say I'm not damaged, that I'm fine. I envy hara like you, because you really are fine. I saw your contempt for me the first minute I laid eyes on you. You see, I have a brain. I have feelings. Sorry to shatter your illusions.'

This conversation had taken a surreal turn. 'No, *I'm* sorry.'

'Don't be. You didn't misjudge me. I tried to take Ysobi off you. I admit that. I do love him, despite what happened. You know what it was like? Rocks cracking, the earth breaking apart. I could hear myself ripping. It was too loud. I felt like I was bleeding inside myself, leaking into every organ. I thought I'd die. It brought it all back, but then Ysobi was there for me, helping me through it. I know I should have told him the history. I didn't want to, because I hate it. So, the answer to your original question is yes, he really hurt me. Is there anything else you want to know?'

Only minutes before, he'd been unable to meet my eyes, now our gazes were locked. 'Did you really try to kill yourself while I was dropping Zeph's pearl?'

'Yes and no. I didn't care if I lived or died, but I wanted Ysobi to stay with me. There were... shadows... in his garden. Sometimes, they'd come right up to the window. I thought they were waiting for me to be alone. It wasn't about love that day. Something else. Does that satisfy you?'

'Have you told anyhar else in Jesith these things?'

'No. I'm only telling you because I know Ysobi's in trouble over me. He shouldn't be blamed. I'm fucked up. I've been thinking how I could tell Sinnar or Tibar, but since you're here, I might as well tell you. They'll send me home, won't they?'

I ducked my head. 'They want a har from Kyme to talk to you first. Sinnar has told Ysobi he mustn't continue with your training.'

'You must be pleased about that.'

I was silent for a moment. 'Has Ysobi been coming here to take aruna with you?'

Gesaril stared at me unabashed. 'He comes to me because I'm afraid. We've taken aruna twice since I've been here. I've hidden from him all that lies inside me. He's been soume for me. He makes me feel better. He's so strong. But then so are you. I can't fight you. I've already told you that. We both tried to curse each other, Jassenah, and it was pointless. I tried to use magic to make Ysobi mine, but it all backfired. It's sad, because I know he could heal me, but it'd take more than just a hienama and student relationship. I got here too late.'

His words actually astounded me. 'I appreciate your honesty, but I think you've played on the fact that Ysobi hurt you and opened you up to these weird hallucinations you're having.'

'Probably. Wouldn't you?' Gesaril laughed bitterly. 'Not that it's got me anywhere. He's tried to help me, but I know he won't risk his position for me. It means more to him than any living har, and that includes you. Like you said, there'll always be students.'

I stood up. 'Thank you for speaking to me. Do you want me to tell Sinnar what you've told me?'

'I suppose you must.' Again, a bleak laugh. 'You must be confused now. I'm pathetic, a creature to be pitied, but I'm also the soume shrew who came between you and Ysobi. Don't bother pitying me. It's not you who's stopping me having him, it's myself. I can't let his reputation be ruined. He means more to me than that. And the fuss you've made means his reputation is hanging by a thread.'

'Actually, it's more than that, Gesaril. This has happened before – twice.'

'I'm not surprised. He's an exceptional har. You can go now. There's nothing else I want to say to you.'

'There's nothing else I want to hear.'

I walked back to town, thinking how right I'd been and also how wrong. Nothing in life is ever simple. It's a tangled web, which gets ever more complex the more closely you examine it. I went to the stone circle in the woods and there sat down. Bluebells were slowly casting a blue shawl across the forest lawn. In this place, I spoke to Aruhani.

His just reward is truth, that's all. I dismiss my anger. Let it be gone.

I then spent some time visualising a healing situation for Gesaril, and it wasn't as difficult as I feared it would be. My anger really had disappeared.

I took the long way round to the Nayati, following paths on the edge of town that kept me away from others.

Aeron and Orphie were both there when I arrived, but Zeph was not. Orphie looked relieved to see me, but also anxious. I said to Ysobi, 'Can we talk now? Or should I come back later?'

Ysobi studied me for some seconds. 'We should

talk now,' he said and turned to his students. 'Carry on. I'll be back shortly.' He directed me into the Nayati itself.

We stood in the empty hall that smelled of incense and wood and the cut greenery that decorated it. Ysobi stood before me with his arms folded, his face expressionless. 'What do you want to say, Jass?'

'Where's Zeph?'

'One of my colleagues has taken him out. He's learning about the forests.'

'Oh. OK.' I paused, took a breath. 'I've been to see Gesaril.'

Ysobi shifted his weight from one foot to the other. 'Did you apologise to him as Sinnar asked?'

'Sort of. I told him he wasn't cursed. Mainly, I asked him some questions.'

'And what evidence did the prosecution uncover, then?'

'That Gesaril was the victim of pelki as a young harling, which has contributed greatly to his current condition.'

Ysobi's eyes widened, and I saw his professional self slip into him at once. 'Really? Is that true?'

'I believe him,' I said. 'It explains a lot. He also confessed to the fact he was – as he put it – trying to take you off me.'

Ysobi put one hand against his mouth for some moments. 'He hid his past well, too well.'

'The hallucinations were real, I think. He sees his attackers. The arunic training must have opened up parts of his mind to such things. He hasn't got over the experience, clearly.'

'Astounding,' Ysobi said. 'And tragic.' He gestured

abruptly. 'Of course: these figures he sees could be thoughtforms, conjured by his own mind.'

I nodded. 'Probably. Well, it lets you off the hook. Gesaril is concerned for your reputation. I don't think he has any intention of returning to the Shadowvales and bad-mouthing your methods, as Sinnar fears. He *is* in love with you.'

Ysobi rubbed his face. 'I didn't intend for that to happen.'

'Maybe not. Look, if you want to go to him, then do. I won't cause any trouble about it. I'm tired of it all. It makes me feel tainted.'

'It wouldn't be fair to go to him,' Ysobi said. 'I can't give him what he wants.'

'You said something similar to me, once.'

'Even if you weren't here, if we'd never happened, I wouldn't go to him, Jass. I never lied to you about my feelings.'

I shrugged. 'Well, whatever. You were right. It seems I can't cope with what you do. I've turned on you, as Morien did, and maybe the one before did too.'

Ysobi considered this. 'It's only Gesaril you can't cope with. I didn't cope with him too well, either. I have a blind spot. I can't see the shadows flying in on me. Sinnar's right. I need to address it.'

'Funny how these shadows have shown up whenever you've taken a chesnari.'

'Perhaps an important lesson.' He paused. 'Where have you been these last few days?'

I held his gaze boldly. 'In the Shadowvales. No, don't look like that. I wasn't searching for evidence about Gesaril. Zehn took me there, as you no doubt know. I needed him, Yz. I needed to try and forget you, because I was so hurt.'

I was gratified by the expression of displeasure that crossed Ysobi's face. 'Was that fair to him?'

'No. Mightily unfair, probably. But Zehn knows the score.'

'And what is that exactly?'

'I can't give him what he wants.'

Ysobi's gaze was unflinching. 'Can you give *me* what I want?'

My heart stilled for a moment. 'I don't know. Can I? What is it you want?'

Ysobi sighed deeply and was silent for some moments, then said, 'What we had. I miss it. Perhaps it was just a dream, after all.'

'No, you're wrong. Chesna isn't a dream. It's gritty and real. It has to be nurtured, maintained and monitored. We didn't do that. It was a mistake we both made.'

'You haven't answered my question.'

'I can't yet,' I said, and I found that that was true. I wanted him more than anything, and yet I could not answer him.

'You know where I am,' Ysobi said. 'It's your call, Jass.'

That night, I could not sleep. Again, the sky was clear and the moon had thinned, although it still provided enough light for me to walk through the fields to think. I wandered out to the cliffs and took the narrow path that followed the line of the coast. I thought about how Orphie and Gesaril had both experienced terrible things when they'd been so young, and how there was so much work Wraeththu still had to do to stop such things from happening. Cursing hara should not be part of the agenda. I was ashamed of how I'd felt before.

I began to retrace my steps, thinking that I might have something to eat before I went to bed. I was beginning to feel slightly drowsy. As I walked, I hummed beneath my breath, but became aware, very slowly, that the atmosphere around me was changing. The night had become still and watchful. I felt unnerved, as I'd felt in the waking dreams that Gesaril had sent to me.

I stopped walking and took an inward reading of the surroundings. I couldn't pick up anything in particular, but had the sense I was no longer alone and that whatever observed me wasn't harish. At once, I started walking again, this time at a quicker pace.

When a white figure ran out of the trees on the hill to my left, I thought at first it was a ghost. It was hurtling towards the cliff edge like a creature possessed. I knew at once it intended to throw itself off, and I didn't care whether it was a ghost or a real har; I had to act. I pelted forwards and hurled myself against the figure, catching hold of its legs so it slammed to the ground. I knelt upright on the body beneath me, aware of various aches in my body from the fall. I knew it would be Gesaril under my knees, and it was.

'What in Ag's name are you doing?' I cried. 'Gesaril?'

He barely seemed aware I was there. His head tossed slowly from side to side, and he uttered groans. He wore only a long nightshirt of thin fabric. His body writhed against the grass, his thighs flexing feebly. It was almost sexual. I became uncomfortably aware of this and climbed off him, tried to lift his upper body in my arms. He lolled heavily, like a sack of stones.

'Gesaril...' I glanced about me. Would I have to carry him back to Jesith?

'I have to...' Gesaril muttered.

'What? Have to kill yourself? Don't be ridiculous.' I wasn't sure what I should say to a suicidal har. I was out of my depth.

'No...' He pressed his cheek against my chest. 'I have to get away from them, and this is the only way.'

'Get away from what?'

Without raising his head, he lifted an arm and pointed behind us. The flesh on my back contracted and I turned swiftly.

'You can't see them, can you?' Gesaril moaned. 'But they're there. *They're there!*

Oh, but I *could* see them. Several tall shadowy shapes that were the essence of menace. They hovered at the edge of a copse of beeches. They watched. 'I see them,' I said. 'I see them, Gesaril.'

Gesaril uttered a sound that was half sob, half laugh. 'You can? But nohar can. They think I'm mad.'

'There are at least five of them,' I said.

Gesaril clutched at my coat. 'I made them,' he gasped. 'I made them from my dreams. I didn't want to, but they won't go away.'

They must have been seven feet tall, mostly without feature, but even so they were hideous. As I stared at them, their grey faces swam in and out of focus; sneering, snarling mouths, dead eyes. They were the rank thoughtforms from a terrified harling's mind; a terrified harling who had been denied his fear, who had been told he was har and therefore would be all right. I was filled with a righteous kind of anger and put Gesaril from me, even though he clawed at me weakly.

'They won't go away?' I said, getting to my feet. 'We'll see about that.'

I took hold of one of Gesaril's hands, pulled upon it. 'Get up, Gesaril. Come with me.'

'No!' He tried to put his arms over his head, but I was stronger than him.

'Trust me,' I said. 'Trust your enemy, for I'm worse than they are!'

I don't know whether it was the steel in my voice that convinced him or whether he was just too tired and frightened to fight me, but he let me drag him over the grass towards his greatest fear.

The apparitions were mindless, entities that had not been properly programmed by Gesaril's feverish imagination other than to loom and torment. They stuck to him because he was their creator. As we approached them, I received no further sense of threat. They were merely watchers, not active beings. Still, it took some courage to actually stand before them, because they were not a part of everyday reality and they were representations of a vile and unforgivable act. I wasn't totally without fear myself, but I was able to focus my intention.

Holding onto Gesaril's hand fiercely, I stared at these creatures and said, 'In the name of Aruhani, I unmake you. In the name of Aruhani, I dismiss you from this realm. Aruhani, Devourer and Creator, take this essence into yourself and consume it. Do it now!'

I then began a chant of Aruhani's name, building it in intensity.

After a few moments, Gesaril's voice joined mine, hesitantly.

I visualised our combined intention as a whirling vortex of cleansing light, and I knew Gesaril saw the same thing. As the energy swirled around us, I connected with Gesaril entirely, fed him with my strength and resolve. I felt him become stronger, and heard his voice become louder. Presently, we were both standing up straight, our voices spiralling as a plait of sound on the night. The shadows before us wavered, became less cohesive. They could not act to defend themselves, because they were just a part of Gesaril, a part he needed to lose. When the power reached a peak, very much like the peak of aruna, we threw up our arms and released it with a wild and furious shout. White light shot out in all directions, which we could almost see with our physical eyes. For a few moments, both my inner and physical sight was blinded, and then I blinked.

Beside me, Gesaril released a ragged laugh. He didn't need to say aloud that his demons had gone.

I took him in my arms and let him weep in relief against me. After a few minutes, he raised his head. 'That was your curse come to life,' he said. 'The power of it. You gave it to me to use.'

'I know,' I replied. I rubbed his bare arms. 'You must be freezing. Come back to my cottage. I'll make you a drink.'

He studied me for a moment, blankly, then nodded once. 'OK.'

Once we were home, I bathed his feet because

they were cut and bleeding. He started to shiver as he sat wrapped in a blanket before my stove, me kneeling before him. 'Why are you doing this?' he asked me.

'It's part of the majhahn,' I answered. 'Just that.'

'You're supposed to hate me,' he said dully. 'In my world, you have to hate me.'

'Who says I don't?' I stood up and tidied away the cloths and water I'd used on his feet. 'I've banished ghosts with you, Gesaril. That doesn't constitute a chesna bond. Lighten up.' I chose those words deliberately, remembering vaguely I'd used them before.

He shook his head and grinned at the floor. 'Can I stay here tonight?'

'Well, the night's nearly gone, but OK.'

Gesaril stretched out his toes towards the stove and pulled the blanket more closely around him, while I set about boiling some water. I barely looked at him, but was conscious of his attention. Eventually he said, 'Jassenah...'

I glanced at him. 'What?'

'I really don't want to have to say this, but...'

I straightened up from my task and stared at him. 'Go on.'

He stared at me for a moment from beneath those dark brows, his full lips slightly open, his hair hanging forward in lush swathes. He was indeed, despite everything, still lovely. 'Ysobi loves you,' he said. 'He's always loved you. Some of the things I said to you...' He shrugged awkwardly. 'I wanted them to be true, but really they weren't. I know he was torn when I begged him to come to me at Sinnar's. I played on his sense of duty. It was wrong. When you left Jesith...'

He shook his head. 'He didn't come to me again. I haven't seen him since. Please don't punish him anymore.'

I was silent for some time as I digested these astonishing disclosures, then ducked my head. 'Thank you.'

'Jassenah...'

'Do you want tea?'

He frowned. 'I *am* sorry.'

'Be quiet. Do you want tea?'

He nodded. 'Yes, please.'

We did not speak again as I made the drinks. When I handed him a hot mug, he held it in both hands. 'They've really gone, those *things*,' he said. 'I think only you could have done that, and only because of what I did to you. It's strange. I think I was meant to come here. I think everything was meant.' He frowned and sipped his drink.

'Work on yourself,' I said. 'Get better. You're young, Gesaril. Your training here has been traumatic, but I agree with you in one respect; what happened might have been the right thing.'

He nodded again and we drank our tea in silence, until the mugs were empty and it was time to go to bed.

I did not, as you might think, initiate some healing and truly altruistic aruna with this damaged har, but I did let him sleep beside me for the rest of the night, and I know his dreams were untroubled.

We'll never be friends, Gesaril and I, but neither will we be enemies. Neither one of us ever mentioned to another har in Jesith what we went through together that night. Sometimes, from Kyme, where he still is, he sends me small gifts; never with a letter or any kind of note, just parcels of herbs or a small carving or a piece of cheap jewellery. In return, I send him, a couple of times a year, a long letter telling him all the news of our small community. I don't know how long this communication will continue.

In the early morning following our impromptu exorcism, and once Gesaril had left my cottage to return to Sinnar's, I went to Orphie's dwelling and posted a note through the door, addressed to Ysobi. All it said was, 'Bring Zeph to me this evening.'

I go back to that evening now; it's as if it were only yesterday, although long years have passed since that time.

I am here in the twilight. Owls swoop across the spreading fields, and the landscape is endless. I am drinking wine that is touched by the chill of evening. I gaze at the bright stars, so many of them. Wondrous pinpricks of light. They are so far from us, incomprehensible and yet, even so, they are ours, because they are eternal. Ever shining.

I want to find the true magic that I know is inside me. I don't want to be a small senseless creature, governed by meaningless fears. I want to rise above it all, to fulfil a potential I have only just begun to imagine. Is it love that hara who are chesnari feel for one another, or something else? What is aruna? Do we misunderstand it so badly, anchoring it to the earth, when it should be part of the sky?

As the dark steals in, I see him standing at the gate. He is tall, like an angel, my son at his side. I wonder how long he has been watching me.

We have a chance, if we can transcend all that we were. We have a chance, if we can understand that the pure born will not be perfect and that Wraeththu is not as far above humanity as it likes to think. We have a chance, if we can become part of the sky.

'Ysobi.' His name.

He opens the gate and they come towards me. Zeph reaches me first. He touches my knee and stares at me with wide pony eyes. 'Jass,' he whispers, '*do.*'

I touch his face and smile. There is such wisdom in his gaze. I stand up.

Ysobi stands before me, almost smiling. 'Here I am,' he says, 'flawed, but decided. My blood is yours, Jassenah, if you'll take it.'

A blood bond: beyond chesna. I bow my head. 'My blood is yours also.'

Ysobi folds his hands about my own. He bends his head to kiss me and his breath tastes of summer. My hienama, my brother, my star.

Other Wraeththu Books from Immanion Press

Student of Kyme
A Wraeththu Mythos Novella
Storm Constantine
9781904853411
£10.99 trade paperback

IP0016 A sequel to The Hienama. The young Wraeththu har, Gesaril, has been shamed and cast out of Jesith, after an inappropriate affair with his hienama, Ysobi. Ysobi's reputation was at stake, so Gesaril was made the scapegoat. Taken in by Huriel Har Kyme, a codexia of the famed Alba Sulh academy, Gesaril vows to begin his life anew in the Wraeththu city of learning. He is determined to put the past and its ghosts behind him, to restore his name and prove to hara he is not what Ysobi painted him to be. But sometimes the past will not lie quietly in its grave, and Gesaril soon learns he must confront the restless ghosts and fight them. Ysobi is not done with him, but no har will believe him. If he is to retain his sanity and his hard won new life, Gesaril must win this bitter war alone, with magic dark and light.

This is a powerful story of obsession, betrayal and doomed love, sure to be a hit with Wraeththu fans and followers of the dark and Gothic alike.

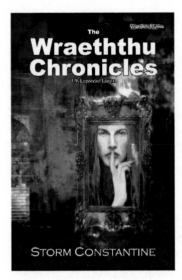

The Wraeththu Chronicles

Omnibus edition of The Enchantments of Flesh and Spirit; The Bewitchments of Love and Hate and The Fulfilments of Fate and Desire

Storm Constantine

1904853293

£16.99 trade paperback

IP0012 The expanded versions of Storm Constantine's ground-breaking trilogy, which first appeared in 1986 and has remained in print ever since. In 2003, Storm re-edited the books, inserting new scenes and reinstating material that was originally cut. These are the author's preferred editions.

Wraeththu have inherited the world from the dying race of humanity. Androgynous, exotic and psychically powerful, they struggle to avoid the mistakes that led to humanity's downfall. But Wraeththu initially derived from humans and carry within them the traits they claim to despise. The trilogy follows the story of the human boy Pellaz who is led to become Wraeththu by the charismatic and enigmatic Cal. Pellaz eventually becomes a figurehead of his people, whereas the doomed Cal trails destruction wherever he wanders. The story of their tragic and fated love has enthralled readers for over twenty years and continues to do so.

Lightning Source UK Ltd.
Milton Keynes UK
06 December 2010

163995UK00001B/24/P